THE LIGHT MAKERS

By the same author

the
LIGHT
MAKERS

mary o'donnell

451
Editions

The Light-Makers
First Edition, 1992
by Poolbeg Press

The Light Makers
2nd Edition
Published by 451 Editions
Dublin
www.451editions.com

ISBN: 978-0-9931443-3-2

Cover and interior design: www.Cyberscribe.ie

Cover photo: www.RawPixel.com

Praise for Mary O'Donnell's work:

ABOUT THE AUTHOR

Mary O'Donnell is the author of fifteen books, both poetry and fiction, and has also co-edited a book of translations from the Galician (See Books Published). Her titles include *Virgin and the Boy*, and *The Elysium Testament*, as well as poetry such as *The Place of Miracles*, *Unlegendary Heroes*, and her most recent critically acclaimed seventh collection *Those April Fevers* (Arc Publications UK, 2015). She has worked in journalism, especially theatre criticism. Her essays on contemporary literary issues are widely published. She also presented and scripted three series of poetry programmes for the national broadcaster RTE Radio, including, during 2005 and 2006, a successful series on poetry in translation called 'Crossing the Lines'. She has taught creative writing at Maynooth University and worked on the faculty of Carlow University Pittsburgh's MFA programme in creative writing for eleven years. She currently teaches creative writing at Galway University. A volume of essays, *Giving Shape to the Moment: the Art of Mary O'Donnell*, *poet, short story writer, novelist* will be published in 2018. She is a member of Aosdána, the multidisciplinary organisation of Irish artists administered by the Irish Arts Council (An Chomhairle Ealaíon).

For more information please see:
www.maryodonnell.com

For Martin, again

Chapter One

—ɯ—

Sam and I used to laugh at our childhoods, not because they were unhappy, which in most respects they weren't, but because like everybody else's they were full of oddity, strange perspectives which made some sense only in hindsight.

My father Daniel married twice. I am a product of the second marriage, my sister Rose of the first union. Both our mothers are now dead. Daniel maintains that most of Rose's problems stem from that time when she faced a schism, when one mother was lost and within eighteen months she had gained another whom she thought she was expected to love. Now he says he might have done things differently.

I would still have married Sam but I would have taken more care. I would have realised that some things are not as important as people imagine. The socially assumed things, the signs of normal human relations—a home, a job, friends, having children—are often surface signals which blink an unreliable message back to the world. All's well, these things assure us. But that's a lie, and we all collude, with too great an energy, in the perpetration of that lie.

The Women's Centre is just another brick-fronted eighteenth-century building. I enter alone, full of self-pity, I whinge and whine constantly about my plight. Without Sam. At least I got myself in here. It's my first time. Half the women in the country seem to attend the place, buying contraceptives, having cervical smears, getting abortion referrals. No, that's not allowed any more. They'd risk having the building burnt down. Not that I've come for any of the gynaecological stuff.

Needs are always hard to admit to. I've managed very well until now; solved all my own problems as Daniel taught me to do years ago. Perhaps I was too well-tutored in the cultivation of outward competence.

"You have to face unpleasant things sometime," he said gently, when once I puked into the sink at the prospect of arithmetic and the teacher who made me re-do my homework every day. I was made to sit on the box which contained a selection of dusters, floor-cleaning powders and thick lumps of wax. Every day. On the rostrum, in front of the class. Daniel did not know about that bit. I used to think I was doing something wrong, that I was bad.

That's how I learnt to face unpleasant things, to stand on my own two feet. It's odd really; ironic that I've come to this, sitting in the waiting-room of the Women's Centre. The woman who will counsel me is engaged with somebody else. Although the walls are quite solid — I know because the first thing I did when I came in was to tap them — I can hear vague murmurings from the next room.

Through the open door I can see young, confident-looking women who bounce up and down the stairs. They seem very friendly, bright, sure of themselves. Their accents are hard to place. One is surely American, east coast; another sounds English but could well be Irish, perhaps a post-graduate student from Trinity doing some kind of research. Was I like that, I wonder? That confident? Ten years ago I was still certain that the world could be changed, that the ignorant and indifferent could gradually be won over, all in the course of my lifetime, to a better kind of civilisation. Now I know that the civilising of human kind needs a slow fermentation, that it take aeons, that in a generation the whole organic mess we call the human race makes a shift towards coherence that is so minuscule as to be virtually invisible. It is a heartbeat, a drop of blood, a breathing-in towards some civilising wholeness but no more than that. Even if I can't change the world, I still believe that certain things can be altered, in spite of the obstinate who allow the rhythm of their lives to harden into stone. However I'm not so sure of myself any more, which is why I'm here.

Another young thing glides past, trips lightly down the stairs, her hair a plummy colour and skin flawless, wearing black leggings and an excuse of a top which hangs loosely over boyish breasts. I'm not even sure how to dress now, and my breasts are big and sloping. Like a landed countrywoman's, Sam used to joke.

Everything about the place is designed to inspire calm and light. The stairs and landings are carpeted in fashionable ropey stuff, the kind you find in some of Sam's houses when the owners furnish them. Bauhaus but not quite. The walls are beige but the paintcard probably calls them oyster or aubade or even magnolia. Etchings and wood-cuttings, surrounded by creamy parchment mountings, framed elegantly in slim black wood, run up along the stairway. It's a Georgian building, the kind that most people don't live in but serve to carry on a business from.

When I came in (after announcing myself through the intercom and waiting until they buzzed the safety-catch on the door), I found that there was a hatch to my left. Again I said who I was.

"Right!" said the cheerful blonde woman within. "You're

11

for Dr Flynn-Mitchell. Go up two flights and turn to your left." she said with a lot of hand movements. She smiled, handing me a card advertising the centre's numerous services. I know the smile is part of her job and I half-resent it, even though it also comforts me in an odd way. I've got out of the habit of expecting smiles for simply being someplace.

On my way up I take in the surroundings: the pictures, the half-landing off which is a white door on which are printed the daunting words, Examination Room. I wonder how many women are examined every year, think of caps and coils, pills, foams and rubbers. Unending streams of women, who had the chance to use them as a matter of course in different phases of their lives! Not like me and Sam, messing about with them for sheer novelty, taking trips to the North years ago to stock up on condoms it turned out we didn't need. Condoms always made me laugh anyway; part of me will never understand why people don't break their sides laughing at them. Probably a matter of urgently not wanting to get pregnant. There's nothing like an unwanted pregnancy to wipe the smile off your face. I remember reading somewhere recently that approximately eighteen million condoms are imported into Ireland annually. Eighteen million mickey-covers on this small island alone! That amounts to one hell of a lot of screwing around. Such statistics can be found in the side columns of newspapers, in blocks of heavy black print.

The English papers are full of tasty morsels of information. "Woman Stoned In Kenya" was one such heading. An infertile woman was singled out by some self-styled messiah who decided she'd been promiscuous and rallied the local people to stone her. She survived and was recovering in hospital in Nairobi. Further snippets include the fact that most Japanese city men have mistresses whom their wives know about, and those same wives are willing to perform blow-jobs on their adolescent sons in order to relieve pre-exam tension in their aspiring offspring. Nine-tenths of the world's illiterate are women; forty-five per cent of First World women will at some time in their lives be unfaithful to their partner. The figure is seventy-five per cent for men.

Finally I reach the counselling floor. A white panelled door marked Psychotherapy and Counselling closes just as I stop to take a breath. I check my watch. Half an hour early at least. Before I can stop myself, I assemble some more scraps of information which, while not concerning me directly, seem nonetheless pertinent. Four thousand women will travel from Ireland to England to have an abortion this year. Our population will be top-heavy with geriatric people by the time the present younger generation has reached old age. That's because my generation, their parents, unlike the rest of Europe, kept on having an average of three to four children. Ha. That's rich. But that's what a lot of people believe. They have children as a kind of insurance policy as much as for any other reason.

Not that I blame them. American television comedy programmes often bring that point up. You see the single woman in search of a man bemoaning her eventual fate — alone, unloved, with nobody to take care of her. That's why single women everywhere are so security-conscious. I've watched them at work and at play. Once they hit thirty they stop taking risks and start saving like blazes because they're all terrified of that word *spinster*, so favoured by the legal profession. It signifies a social blight, a feeling of being unwanted, of spinning away at threads of empty time.

Magazines lie strewn on the coffee-table in the waiting-room. Copies of *Spare Rib, Options, Image, Business & Finance* (a deliberate gesture, the Centre's way of saying that it realises that many of the women attending have climbed to the top of what is now called the "corporate ladder.")

I sit with my hands folded in my lap. My heart is beating quickly. I don't want another panic attack. That's the last thing I need. I instruct myself to be calm. Useless. Tell myself that I am not going to keel over and die, that even if I do, what of it? If there is something on the other side, all my troubles are over. If there isn't, I won't be any the wiser because I'll be dead anyway.

At least there's nobody around to observe this panic. My heart is going to burst from its cage and take flight. My stomach has burned itself to a cindery knot. I am taken over, controlled by it. I deliberately dig my nails into the palms of my hands. If I can draw blood, if I can create real physical pain, that will help to absorb my attention. Is there no one to take me on? Is there no one to relieve me, to help? Must it always be like this? Must I always be strong and brave and competent? Am I never to be allowed simply to curl up and stop trying? I want to kick and scream, scratch my own face; I want the relief of real pain, because after pain comes ease and perhaps oblivion. Finally I draw blood. The nails of my right hand have burst through the soft skin below the flesh pad at the base of my thumb. I snivel like an idiot, my face hot, my chest tight as a plastic bag filled with water. I would like to explode with self-pity. It's not fair. It's damn well not fair. This was never part of the plan. I rise and pace back and forth, wipe my bleeding hand along my white jacket. Deliberately. The white and perfect must be sullied, light spun to darkness. Nothing is to be trusted.

I catch sight of myself in the octagonal mirror provided by the Centre. I am, in spite of my black rage and terror, horrified.

Is this what it has come to? My new slenderness, my

14

thick, wavy brown hair (not a grey rib to be seen), my well-made looks, I am attractive enough. I can see myself and how others must superficially regard me. Part of me, maybe the sane bit that's left, the vestige of the sassy kid I used to be years ago, is objective enough to regard the form in the mirror. I weep aloud; my mouth hangs ludicrously open, wet and horrible; my neck is blotchy. I want to be absorbed by the world. Whether that means living or dying is beyond me. I don't care so long as it brings some sort of peace. For the umpteenth time I wonder how I got into this mess, feel life well up around me like a dangerous pool, life as I have lived it, swirling, sucking, threatening. Soon I will be submerged. I can forget Sam, Rose, Daniel. And the Frenchwoman. I can forget the yob who almost gave me the sack last week but didn't because I gave him the hard sell that his damn newspaper needs someone like me, that I'm the best there is even if he doesn't realise it, that I'm in demand as no other photographer has ever been before. Some part of me believes that. But today it's a fiction I concoct in order to survive.

Today I would gladly toss a hand-grenade into the darkroom, booby-trap every word processor in the place, release viruses into the system and put cyanide in the newsroom coffee. Today I could whip Sam till his flesh was red-raw. Today I could murder him and that woman.

But help is on hand. At least I am not stoic and see no reason to endure what is making me ill. I thirst. If I were a character in the Bible (Old Testament), or a film, something would happen. Light would come through darkness, trees would bloom, birds would sing. I think of manna falling on the desert, of honey made by wild bees, of Ingrid Bergman and things happening on cue (just when you need them and not when every ounce of resilience and tolerance has been wrung from your mind).

The door of the counselling-room opens and another face appears. It must be Dr Flynn-Mitchell. She's slim, wire-haired and pleasant-looking. I make no attempt to dry my eyes. They're so puffy it wouldn't make any difference.

"You must be Hanna Troy," she greets me in a whispering voice. She is apologetic too. "I'm so sorry, but would you mind terribly coming back in three hours?" she asks, bending towards me solicitously.

"No. No problem. I can come back later," I mumble. I'm free. Nothing doing but a photo-call at the Contemporary Image Centre the following morning.

"You're sure about that now? We can always get somebody else to see you immediately, if you want."

"Just give me a time and I'll come back. I can wait."

"Say, five to five-fifteen?" she suggests. "It's just that I'm going to be longer than expected — I really am sorry. You *will* come back, won't you?"

"Definitely. Five o'clock so," I say.

She must be in the middle of a heavy session. I have no difficulty understanding that kind of thing. Inconsistencies. Last-minute cancellations because somebody else is having a brainstorm. In a way it increases my confidence in Dr Flynn-Mitchell. If she's prepared to change appointment times at the drop of a hat, bend to the unexpected to that extent, that must mean she can accommodate all sorts of problems and hear them out.

I have stopped trembling. Having seen Dr Flynn-Mitchell, I am calmer. She looks reassuring. I hesitate for at least five minutes before deciding what to do. Whether to wait and flick through magazines for hours on end and probably keep thinking the very worst as regards the future, or whether to take a stroll through the city to kill time. Because time must be killed if it is not filled satisfactorily. Every decision is major these days. Then my body is off the chair, without any apparent decision, and I know that I'll walk down Leeson Street. Whether I'll head in the direction of the canal or in the direction of St Stephen's Green is another thing. I'll wait until I'm on the street. I'm good at killing time. At waiting. On the street the bricks on the buildings opposite seem deliciously clear, lit by an early afternoon translucence, the faintest of shadows falling from the grouting between them, casting hints of darkness across the murky pinks and browns.

Chapter Two

—ʍ—

The sky is the bluest blue I can imagine. I wonder if my mother will ever find material like that. I'd like her to make me a dress of summer sky blue. I am impossibly happy and know it, as I sit with my back to an oak tree, a blank jotter on my knee and colouring crayons scattered in the grass. Rose's voice is somewhere in the distance, high-pitched and imperious. She's arguing with Kate, my mother, her stepmother. She is five years older and knows everything, even if she does fight a lot with Kate. We call our parents Kate and Daniel because Rose has always refused to call Kate Mother and so for the sake of making things equal we never refer to Daniel as Daddy either.

I squint at the picture just drawn. It's one of a series of houses. I like drawing houses. Most of them are the same and totally unlike our own. A square first, then a line to the right, top and bottom. I join these two lines and put a triangle on top. This is followed by another line leading from the top of the triangle, and a slanting one which comes down to join the far side of the square.

I consider myself quite clever to have discovered how to draw the gable-end as well as the front of a house. Rose says it's called perspective. Per-spek-tiv. I repeat the word aloud, amused at the sound. A difficult word for something simple. The windows are four smaller squares which I colour in with frilly red curtains. The door is a rectangle on which I place a round doorknob and a horseshoe-shaped knocker. A curving path swirls from the doorway to the gate, which is crossed with an X to indicate wooden cross-beams. Sometimes there are trees, plump, billowy forms, always in leaf. And seagulls. The easiest birds of all to draw. We live thirty miles from the sea, just inside the border at Clonfoy, within the piece of the county that juts up and is surrounded by Northern Ireland. But the big lake is just down the hill from the house, Tongs Lough.

I see it every day, check it automatically for changes in colour. I know, for example, that if it's dead calm and green, we're in for a storm, and if the surface ripples slightly in the breeze, the colour a light grey-blue, the weather will hold. The gulls swoop and dive, little herring-gulls that make a silvery cut of sound as they circle the shore. Two small curved things suggest a gull in my picture. That's another discovery which leads me to believe I'm rather clever.

It's the kind of house I'd like to live in. Ours is older than the houses in the town. My friends live in townhouses. Most of their homes look alike, something of which I approve. Our house isn't like any I've seen before. It's plastered with old grey stuff; the windows are long, white-painted and arch to a narrow point, and the door is also white. A glass panel rises on each side and then curves round the top of the door. It has stained-glass flowers, exotic birds, tendrils and curlicues that weave in and out of the lead-lattice. A clematis plant which Dan's first wife planted years beforehand has now grown vigorous and competes with the wild roses on the other side of the entrance to the house. It is so ambitious that the tiniest youngest tendrils have begun to bloom for the first time just below my bedroom window, and robins and wrens nest there, close to the wall.

"That's because it's warm," says Rose. "The front of the house catches the sun."

Touching a nest, or interfering in any way with her eggs, is one of the greatest crimes anybody could commit. Almost the same as saying the word "fuck." My parents only laugh the day I come home from school and say that someone has written the word "fuck" in giant chalky letters on the playground. What does it mean? Can I use it? It sounds so definite, so sharp and final that I wander around for a couple of hours going *fuck-fuck-fuck-fuck-fuck-fuck-fuck*...But although they find it amusing, they say that I must never, ever use that word because it's bad. As bad as sucking gobstoppers? More or less, Kate concedes, smiling. The bogeyman follows children who suck gobstoppers. So Rose says. And he chokes them before the gobstoppers can do the job first. And then you go to hell where the Devil shoves a red-hot poker down your throat every day for all eternity.

Nevertheless I take an egg from a robin's nest. This one's not in the clematis but further down the garden, tucked secretly into a shrubby bank. I've never been so close to a nest, can hardly believe my luck. I peer and peer, agog at the cosiness — all that twining and the fluffed lining of grey feather. It is too much. Just one egg will do no harm. My secret. I place the egg carefully in the pocket of my gingham dress, go to my room and hide it in tissue at the back of the wardrobe.

The garden is one of my favourite places.

"Don't you get bored?" friends ask occasionally when we play after school in the yard behind my grandmother's townhouse. But I don't get bored, or not often. There's the garden to explore, trees to climb, and dogs to play with. I try to draw Bobby. He's the bigger one. But it's no good. He won't stay still and I can only draw stationary objects like houses and flowers and trees and the moon.

20

"The moon isn't really still," says Rose.

"But it is!" I insist.

"No it isn't—you just think it is. It's always moving round the earth, just like the earth's always moving around the sun."

"Why?"

"I don't know. Do ya have to know the whys and wherefores of everything?"

"Yes."

Rose rolls her eyes impatiently. "It's got to do with gravity—and don't ask me to explain that because you wouldn't understand it anyway," she says in a superior tone.

On Saturdays I go to the creamery with Daniel.

"Don't just say he works there," says Rose. "He *manages* it."

"What does that mean?" I ask.

"He looks after things—he keeps it going—he's the boss, dummy!"

The creamery sounds terrifying. The clanking of empty milkchurns can be heard even where we live, nearly a mile up the road. It's a cream-coloured pebble-dash building divided into two main sections. Is it cream because they make cream or cream because it's painted cream? On summer mornings at about ten o'clock a regular creaking sound can be heard passing along the road below the house, as the last donkey and cart in the area heads for the creamery with three churns behind the farmer. It is 1963 and everybody else drives a tractor and trailer, or vans, or in an emergency loads the churns into the boot of an Austin or even the back seat of the car. I have occasionally had lifts home from school with farmers whose cars stank of sour milk and sheepwool.

Daniel checks the ledgers on Saturdays, looking up the

names of farmers whose milk has not passed the methylene blue test or noting the weekly statistics for salt and moisture levels in the butter. the methylene blue test reminds me of diphtheria injections and tooth extractions and people leaning over your body, doing things which are for your own good.

"What happens to the farmers if they don't pass the methylene blue test?"

"Nothing," Daniel replies absently, totting up something, his pipe sticking at an angle from his mouth.

"But it's a test! What happens if they fail it?"

"It's not the farmers that fail the test; it's their milk," he murmurs. The world is crazier than I'd thought. Milk passes or fails tests. The moon actually moves, and the sun doesn't.

I follow him to the dairy. It is noisy and metallic-sounding. It smells very sweet and resh with thousands of gallons of milk an great vats of frothy cream. There's so much milk in there that you could take a swim, I tell Daniel.

"Best not," he says seriously, though his eyes crinkle, "unless you want to be like Cleopatra, except she bathed in asses' milk."

I watch him talk with the men on the platform. He seems to know everything, and they appear to like him. That doesn't surprise me. My father is the most wonderful man in the world, knows everything, can drive and swim and buys us great books. He is also, importantly, incapable of keeping an eye on either Rose or me at home. He sits smoking, reading or watching television, and in Kate's absence we undertake great feats of cookery, make lurid green peppermints and sticky toffee but have the mess cleared up before she returns.

After watching the milk for a while, we go through to the butter-making section of the dairy. He points out the new machine which arrived from Germany a few weeks before.

This machine is obviously important and Daniel is delighted with it.

"We'll have fun getting this one underway," he tells me.

"It's very shiny," I remark.

"It'll make better butter and it'll make packing easier," he answers. "We might even win the Read Cup next year — with any luck."

It's like a huge, steel animal, all limbs and protrusions from a vat-like centre.

"See — the cream goes in here," Daniel points to a large opening, "and comes out here as butter." He points to the other end of the machine. I am impressed. The butter snakes out in a thick, smooth runnel and oozes into the waiting boxes. It comes out slowly, which gives the men time to pack it in firmly and slide the next box under the cold, creamy lava. The smell is the freshest, sweetest, imaginable.

We stroll out from the dairy and into the boiler-room. The man who stokes the fire is all chat. He and my father begin to admire the boiler. It's an old one which the previous manager had almost got rid of but Daniel, who was assistant manager then, persuaded him to get it repaired. Jimmy McAteer is the boilerman. He wears an overall smeared thickly with grease and coal-dust, and a shiny cap tilted to one side. Underneath, his hair is grey and shiny, his skin swarthy and brown. There's a thick grime beneath his nails and his hands are coarse. I like him too. He always has a mint sweet in the depths of his pockets. The pair of them stand admiring the boiler as if it is the greatest machine ever.

Outside, the cooling system roars as water gushes down horizontal rows of rusted pipes. Things grow on those pipes, creepy-looking things you wouldn't want to touch. But the creamery on Saturday morning is the place to be. Different from school, different from home, where Rose is still in bed or up washing her hair, and where Kate is baking bread in a cloud of flour, her brow set as she adds buttermilk to the hole in the centre of the bowl.

Not that my mother is a particularly homely kind of person. She comes from a family not much given to fussing over practicalities, although there's a side to them that is full of curiosity about the world. If she had her life to live all over again, she says she would have been an actress or a singer and would have made people call her Katherine and not Kate. She has two brothers alive and two sisters. One brother was killed in Egypt during the war and the other died of a heart-attack. She tells us about the letters Marius used to write home. He was a bad letter-writer who couldn't spell properly, but those letters mean the world to the Bardons. We enjoy everything she tells us about the war years. Quite often she tells us things on a Saturday, and even Rose is not too grown-up to listen and does not make a point out of the fact that Kate is not her real mother.

"There used to be great crack in our house," Kate will say. She comes from a village in the Bragan valley, six miles from Clonfoy, where her father was a cattle-dealer. Her brothers had odd-sounding names like Joachim, Marius, Ross and Theo. Her sisters are called Florence and Nellie, the former after Florence Nightingale because her mother had read a life of the nurse who saved lives out in the Crimea and never forgot the butchery of war. Nellie was called after Nellie Melba, the great Australian opera-singer who now had a dessert named after her—peach Melba. When I ask Kate who is *she* named after, she replies that it's probably some character in a book too.

"Katherine Mansfield perhaps," she says in hopeful tones. Her mother used to read her way through her pregnancies.

"Why?" asks Rose.

"It helped her forget herself."

"Why would she want to do that?"

"It's hard to explain—you only know when it happens to yourself," she says, flattening out a mound of raw brown-bread mixture with floured knuckles.

"When what happens?" says Rose, deliberately persistent, curiosity egging her on.

"When you get pregnant."

Rose and I exchange looks, for once bridging the difference in our ages. Kate has mentioned the P-word again. We say nothing for a while. My sister's eye rests dreamily on the baking-tin, and we watch as Kate cuts a shallow cross through the bread with a knife.

"I'm never going to get pregnant," she says then firmly.

"Neither am I," I add in imitation. Kate smiles.

"Course you will," she says lightly, lifting two tins from the table and checking the oven temperature.

"Babies are disgusting," says Rose.

"All that gook and pee!" I add with bravado.

"You'll get over that; there's worse than gook and pee," says Kate.

"Anyhow," she adds, "that's all years ahead, and who knows what could happen between now and then? You girls have such opportunities nowadays and you can't beat a good education."

"It's easily carried," Rose and I chant, familiar with Kate's views on education.

Over the years we have had much more to do with her family than with Daniel's. For one thing, his people come from Munster, which makes visiting awkward. We meet our relations on Kate's side practically every week. Most of them, like her, have moved closer to the big town, have their own husbands, wives and large families. Ours is the smallest on her side. The others have families of four, five, six and even seven children. Hardly a year passes without our hearing that some aunt or distant cousin has gone into Maple Hill nursing home. Kate's other sister, Aunt Nellie, emigrated to New York when she was twenty and hadn't been home since. My grandmother sends her a copy of the *Border Celt* every week and Nellie writes uninformative scraps of letters every so often. She talks about things, about the price of food, clothes and apartments, but never about people. Once, I write and ask her what the Hudson River is like and a line of reply is addressed to me in that year's Christmas card. She says it's a big river but filthy and only blacks swim there. Sometimes she sends home huge boxes of clothes which nobody really needs, odd-looking dresses which close with strips of Velcro, trousers with double-seats, and gaudy velvet things for the grown-ups. It's so long since she's been home that she has forgotten how we live, Kate says, but she insists that Rose and I write to thank her for her kindness and trouble.

During the war one of the boys, usually Joachim, would buy different newspapers every few days. The whole family enjoyed following Hitler's progress and for a long time cheered him on his way as the German army bit into Czechoslovakia, Poland and Austria. My mother was friendly with an Italian family in her village and learnt the Fascist anthem by heart from their youngest daughter. Theo spoke some German and explained that *Lebensraum* meant space to live in, more room for living, and that that was only Hitler's excuse, even after Neville Chamberlain came back to England waving his bit of paper in the breeze.

"Yon buck's up to no good," Ross would say over his boiled egg and toast. Ross was the youngest boy and stayed at home to work with his father. When he wasn't buying or selling cattle at the marts or finally loading the beasts for live export, he was in church. Ross was always religious, according to Kate, really gospel-greedy, running to benediction and men's sodalities, Mass every day, confession every Saturday come hell or high water. Kate disapproves of religion, even though she attends church herself.

"He was very good-living," she tells us. Ross died young, of a heart-attack.

"There he was in church one day, saying his prayers and minding his own business when it struck. Just like that."

Kate's eyes filled with tears at the thought of it. Ross was everybody's favourite. He'd never have married. There was something old-fashioned about him from the word go.

"Maybe God had an eye on him, wanted him for himself," Kate says.

I do not know what "good-living" means. It is said of men and women who attend church frequently. But I know from experience that some of the very ones running up and down aisles can be terrors. Our aunt Florence is an example.

"She's no Florence Nightingale," says Rose derisively, leaning across the table that Kate is trying to wipe clear of flour.

"By God, she wouldn't agree with you," says Kate, laughing. We know that deep down Florence isn't the kind of person Kate particularly likes, even if she is her sister, and that secretly she's as pleased as hell that Rose has been so perceptive.

"Why's she always going to mass?" I ask.

"Because she's religious," Kate replies evasively.

"She has lovely jangly rosary-beads."

"Ay, that'd be Florrie all right — all set to sparkle whatever the occasion," says Kate, forgetting herself.

Florence is the family glamour girl. She dresses in bright colours, wears heavy gold earrings and laughs a lot. I do not like her laughter. It sounds as if she is trying to let people see how good-humoured she is, how pleasant. Sure enough, her cackle attracts attention. People look intently at her, often with admiration, sometimes with amusement. She is Rose's godmother. Not the kind you read about in fairytales. For her Holy Communion day she bought Rose a blue and white statue of Our Lady and a pair of pink rosary-beads. She is very correct. She reports things to our mother, talks endlessly on the phone about our cousins, who live beside her just outside the town. What time they come home from dances; who they're with; how long they spend in the car. She is scandalised to find one of the girls arriving home at six o'clock one summer morning in her boyfriend's car.

Florence married well. That means she married a man with money. They have six children and a woman who helps in the house. Because she has six children, my uncles are particularly solicitous of Florrie. They think she's done something marvellous and phone her regularly or drop in to see her. She is tall and black-haired and, despite having had six children, she still looks young. Not like some of the women around the town. They move slowly, puffy and shapeless, their children messy-looking, faces sticky with ice-pops and toffee.

"It's hard to look nice when you're poor," Kate says. "You can't afford anything for yourself and you're always tired unless you have help."

Chapter Three

—w—

I head down towards St Stephen's Green and pass a photographer's studio on the way. Vaguely I recall an Easter when first I wanted to become a photographer. Uncle Theo had the knack of catching people off-guard and yet could create a sense of unity in his pictures. Even then, he had a camera which could be set on a timer, giving him the chance to be included in the composition. He always ended up rushing back to the group while the timer pipped, which guaranteed smiles all round from everybody as they watched him slide down on his knees near the front, out of breath and full of good humour. Dan has those old photographs in a box somewhere, wrapped in blue tissue-paper, each one kept separate and safe from light. Odd that. How light, which brings a photograph into being in the first place, eventually corrupts its own creation. Some people would pay big money for Uncle Theo's photos: the ad agencies, programme makers, television people, historians. But they're worth more than money and Dan knows that. Someday I'll piece them together, will write the script that goes with Uncle Theo's photographs. The story of an unexceptional family whose main claim to fame was that they existed in the twentieth century and suffered all its divisions.

I am a product of the past but the roots of that past would seem to have vanished, submerged by a present which has hurtled out of control. It would be good to feel in control again. This city is a place I have always been comforted by; yet it too fails me. The photographer's window is crammed with visual tricks: bridal scenes, conferrings, a few simple studies, a few ghastly ones of coy children trained to sit like performing animals. Soft focus is *de rigueur*. Hazy borders, double exposures. I catch sight of my expression in the window. My lip is curling and I look serious.

I have just observed one of the most popular poses: the bride and bridegroom gaze adoringly at her rings, their faces misty. Who concocts this nonsense? Who sells us so short in matters of love? At least Sam and I didn't go in for the total performance on our wedding-day. Not for us the pathetic jumping through hoops for the sake of appearances. A friend took the pictures, good crisp ones. He didn't cajole me to smile. As I look back I think now that it might have been better had he done so, I was going through my serious phase and was damned if I was going to giggle and simper just because I wore a long white dress and veil. One thing about Sam was that he didn't take himself so seriously in those days. He had the knack of forgetting himself, of forgetting what others thought. Well, in most respects. In later years, he couldn't forget himself at all.

Chapter Four

During the war Kate says she and Joachim would go to the station in Clonfoy every Saturday, just to watch the people from north of the border arrive on the train. There were shortages of all kinds on the other side. By that time she was sixteen and accompanied Joachim only because of the possibility of spotting Mr Right. Mr Right is the sort of man all women dream about.

"Well, did you see him?" I drawl, without having a clue what "Mr Right" really meant.

"Yes and no," she answers. Nothing is clearcut with Kate. There are at least two sides to every situation, something she likes to make clear in every conversation and argument.

"I saw this really handsome fellow get off the train," she says. He was taller than any man she had seen before.

"But it wasn't just his height. He was the best-looking fellow I'd ever clapped eyes on, like Gregory Peck and Trevor Howard all mixed up," she says dreamily.

"Did you get to meet him?"

She thinks for a minute. "Not for years afterwards. Then it was at a party. He'd never have remembered me anyway. He was a painter. Still is, in fact."

"I'm never going to get married," I state, just for something definite to say and to keep the chat going.

"Who'd have you anyhow?" Rose cuts in.

"Oh there'll be plenty will have her when the time

comes. Whatever about the babies, she'll go off with someone sooner or later, and probably sooner than is good for her!" Kate replies in scorn.

"How did Marius die?" Rose asks. Both of us know how he left home when he was sixteen and went to England looking for work. Marius hated school, and used to talk about how when he was a man he was going to make something of his life, without bloody arithmetic.

"Mother was always at him about his language," says Kate.

"What language? Bloody?" Rose asks incredulously.

"Things were different then. There was less effing and blinding."

He joined the British army as a private and ended up in Egypt. There were five letters from him before he died. Kate has all five, which she keeps in her jewel-box. Every so often we take them out and have a good read. She doesn't mind as long as we're careful and put them back in the little plastic bag. What I like about them are the familiar things he mentions, things we might recognise at home.

BFPO 42

Dear All,

How are you? Well, today finds me not so far from Alex. Got yr resent letters, thank all conserned and tell Florrie I'll bring her back some stones for jewlery. They're cheep here and I can purchize them eazily. The air is very dry and believe it or not I miss the rain. I never knew the swallows came to these parts, sure enough here they are, swoopin and divin even tho there isn't much to see but sand. Are yez going to Blackrock this summer? I don't think I'll get leave before Sept.

Kate you would like it here, the sun's always shinin and there's some right quare fellas dressed up in outfits that look like dresses.

You could paint them and you could take camel rides. Some of the Arabs give these animals a name, like we'd give to people. I took a ride on one last month. It was called Fatima. That's all for now. Keep writin. It gets quite here at nights. We're expectin the worst soon. Hope yer not still cheerin for Hitler. Read the Manchester Guardian if yez want to find out what's really happenin to the Jews. Never mind that eejit Haw-Haw. Bye for now,

Marius XXXXXX

Kate says that Marius was no fool, even if he couldn't spell. Words aren't everything; it's what they mean and what you mean using them that counts.

"That was poor Marius," she sighs.

When Marius was killed and then two years later when Ross dropped dead in the church, our grandmother went into a decline. She lost interest in the smart hats with broad brims, the nipped-in waists, the neat little shoes and astrakhan collars of which she was so fond. Kate says it was because her heart had broken. I imagined it cracking loudly, fractured like a heart shaped of solid rock, falling apart like the heart of the prince in Oscar Wilde's story when the little swallow dies. "Poor Marius," Kate still says every so often.

We have been told that swallows come back to the same place every year. It is incomprehensible but I want it to be true. When Kate talks about Marius, I wonder if the swallows that nest in our eaves have by any chance flown all the way from El Alamein and the desert outside Alexandria. In spite of the dry air that Marius mentioned, I think of Egypt as a place where the light is soft and silken and the sky turquoise, with pyramids and sphinxes to beat the band and the desert stretching like sun-tinted pink powder as far as the horizon.

Chapter Five

—⁓—

Even at the beginning of the investigations, when the test should have been done on him, he was reluctant. Even then he denied the possibility. I turn from the photographer's window. They are all so young, these brides and grooms, and at thirty-five I feel so old. This is patent nonsense, I tell myself, thinking of the dynamic fifty-year-olds who exude energy, the trail of divorcees one hears of, women who are never too old to fight the good fight.

Young people in their early twenties irritate me. No doubt this stems from a mixture of faint jealousy and huge regret on my part. At the traffic lights on the Green I watch them. They are jittery and restless, young men with short glossy hair, ties loosened during the warm lunchbreak, who head into the park with burgers in hand and headphones on ears. By the look of their suits I judge the group to be composed mainly of accountants. They are sewn into fashionably loose navy pinstripes with requisite braces. Loose they may be, fashionable, but the pinstripe is intact; they are stamped with the insignia of the future big money-earner.

I follow them into the park, drifting aimlessly, concentrating on looking normal. Even if my mind is scarified, I can make an effort with appearances. I imagine the lives of such men. So predictable. I do not resent the course that most people's lives inevitably take. What irks is the knowledge that the majority will take for granted what Sam and I could not. They will marry young fillies of women, university-educated like themselves. The women will work for two or three years before getting pregnant. There will be gasping, delighted phone conversations with the girls as the news is relayed. Mothers and mothers-in-law will be informed. Every step of the way monitored by clever photographs, as the video cameras whir. All for replay in future years, to stir memories and amuse or mortify the by then half-grown offspring.

How we distort light! How we pervert our human image by clever camera-work! It is my speciality. I have seen them all – socialites, actors, writers, editors, business people – only too delighted to have me create an image that is not really theirs, for some newpaper, magazine or poster. There is nothing wrong with any of it. Nothing whatsoever. It's the ones who take it all for granted that bother me. Those who assume it is theirs by right.

Chapter Six

—⚏—

Sam's people come from a village four miles away from Clonfoy, where his father minds the horses at an equestrian centre run by the local gentry. Even in 1967, when I first meet Sam, much of what happens in the village is determined by life behind the elegant screen of trees, beyond the high, ruckled stone wall. It is a marvellous, scandalous place and I run into him by sheer chance one day at the end of the hunting season. The harriers from the next county have joined with our lot for the day and have headed off across the wide fields, taking Dan and Kate for their first serious hunt. Neither rides particularly well, but they manage to stay on in a bumpy way, feet sticking out awkwardly as they sit astride their horses, backs uneasy and too slumped. Rose has brought me along more as an excuse than anything else. She is keen to chat up one of the stable-boys and I am merely a prop in her private drama. By the time she locates the object of her affection, I have grown bored standing behind as she laughs and giggles with a boy who is ugly with adolescence.

The word *discotheque* rumbles around my head as I wander away from her. According to Kate discotheques are the latest thing sweeping England and France, places where people get together and dance to modern music, where there are no foxtrots and quicksteps, not even rock 'n' roll, and you don't have to be young. They're for everybody, Kate says. She and Dan will attend their first discotheque in the castle grounds that night, after the hunt, having decided that Rose is also old enough to go but that I am not.

I wander away from my sister, disconsolate at this exclusion, longing for excitement and noise, laughter, the aroma of French cigarettes which the types attending this discotheque will surely be smoking. Cutting through the trees between the stables and the castle I mutter to myself — curse and swear in a way I would not dare in front of people, *fuck-fuck-fuck-fuck-fuck-bitches-bastards-fuckthemanyway-thelotovthem-fuckemall*, working through an angry rhythm as I move, hopping over ferns and twigs, avoiding the path that the horses' hooves have churned to muck. In the distance somebody crouches before the castle. I cannot see what he is doing but he is absorbed, his head darting up and down at intervals. Out of curiosity I approach, deciding automatically that if he looks towards me, I shall say hello; if not, I shall ignore him and walk past on the pretext of simply taking a stroll through the grounds.

As I cross the grass, I stop to clean the muck off my boots. White, leather high-boots to match a white miniskirt. The sound attracts his attention; he turns, his face unsmiling and even irritated. He is not so much older than me, a boy of Rose's age or less, and now that he straightens, I see that he has been sketching the castle. He nods cautiously in my direction.

"Hello," I say in response, taking the nod as an invitation to join him. As I approach, he slams the sketchbook closed, his mouth creasing in a tight smile which is not very reassuring.

"Did you not go on the hunt?" he asks diffidently, not looking at me directly.

"No. I don't like horses — well, that is to say, I like them but I get a bit afraid."

"Nothing to it," he says dismissively but his smile has warmed a bit. I stare and stare at the sketching-block across his lap, reluctant to ask him what he's about.

"It's just a drawing," he says in answer to my silent question.

"What of?"

"The castle. I'm practising."

"What for?"

"College."

"Where?"

"Dublin I suppose."

"You're going to be an artist?"

"An architect," he replies with a shake of his head.

I like this boy. He is thickset, not exactly good-looking, but robust, unlike the gosling whom Rose is wasting her time with. His hair is thick and brown and glossy, his skin sallow, the eyes greenish-brown, depending on whether he looks at me, facing the sun, or away towards the castle, when they appear browner. His nose has a slight bump and above his right eyebrow there is an old scar.

"Show me your picture!" I burst out suddenly, full of admiration for him.

"Naw, you wouldn't want to see that."

"Go on, show me!"

To my surprise he opens the sketchbook. What he has drawn is an exact replica of the castle. I am amazed to see the fluted columns of limestone reflected so unerringly, the jutting turrets, the lead-latticed windows and rising battlements. Not only that but he has produced the texture of the stonework as well. For a moment, the image on the page is more glaringly real, more habitable, more desirable than the castle itself. It is the sort of place where this boy and I could live, a forever-and-ever palace where we would draw, and dance and play together, in rooms slashed with the brilliance of sunlight, warm and bright.

"It's very good," I say shyly, afraid he'll think I'm sucking up to him if I say more, or that I don't really mean it.

"It's better than others I've done, getting better every time."

He tells me his name is Sam Wright and that he knows who I am.

"I know your surname anyway," he says. "You're Rose Troy's sister." He smiles knowingly.

"Hanna," I reply. I offer my hand, then withdraw it, feeling the gesture to be absurdly unfashionable. Our hands pause in mid-air, then drop hurriedly.

"I have an Aunt Hanna lives in Belfast. She's a bookbinder."

I am at a loss for a reply, scarcely knowing what a bookbinder does.

"You going to this disco thing?" he asks, closing the sketchbook once again.

"Have you finished it?"

I'm afraid I have disturbed him at some vital moment of inspiration. He nods, putting away his pens and inks, stuffing his pockets with them.

"No. Not allowed," I finally answer his question.

"You're not missing much anyway," he informs me confidently. "A whole load of people jumping and prancing and getting drunk and smoking things."

"French cigarettes?" I press, eager for information on the goings-on of our elders.

"Worse," he says.

"You mean *drugs*?" I am aghast.

"People live differently here," he tells me casually, filling me in on the lord of the manor's first wife, an artist of some

40

kind whom he divorced in favour of a second, younger woman.

"*She* had an abortion."

"Who? The first one?"

"The second one."

"And they got divorced?"

"The first one, not the second one—in England. No problem to them. They have money."

Sam tells the most fantastic stories. He likes having me listen but he is not an eager or easy conversationalist. Everything he says is measured and probably highly accurate, which leaves me thinking that his snippets of information are all the more valuable indeed. He stands up, gathers his pens and the writing block, and we drift slowly out from the castle towards the main gates. In the distance the thunder of horses' hooves can be heard; the hounds are baying. It is an early spring day. Rose laughs somewhere on the other side of the trees, her high-pitched, madly giddy crescendo rising over it all.

"Want a mineral?" Sam asks suddenly as we wander up the deserted main street on the other side of the gates. I sit outside a public house on a blue bench, and a few minutes later he appears with a tray and two bubbling glasses of chilled Cidona. We sit and sip. I try not to gulp; want to appear cool and mature. I cross my legs and a silence falls between us. It is an easy silence, disturbed only by chattering rooks in the yew trees, an odd fly buzzing past in the new-year warmth, muffled sounds from within the pub.

Suddenly the peace of the mid-afternoon is shattered by horn-blowing in the distance, the sound of cars approaching at high speed, a lot of bumping and screaming and yelping. Sam moans and puts his hand to his forehead.

"What's wrong?" I ask.

41

Behind us the public-house windows have been flung open and the heads and shoulders of some of the drinkers appear. Their faces are amused and anticipatory.

"It's a stag," he groans, rolling his eyes.

"What's that?"

Before he can reply, the cars rumble up the hill from our right. Attached to the first vehicle is a trailer and a naked man is bound up with rope in the back of it. They have plastered the front of his body with a shiny black substance, either tar or paint. His hair is spiked and sticky, his face unrecognisable. He sits there, being bumped around, without protest, as if he must endure the episode.

"G'won outta that, ya fuckin' hoor!" a man behind screams from the pub. The others join in, baying and screaming like hounds. Sam and I sit quite still.

The cars turn at the bottom of the village and as they come up towards us again I see what I had not initially noticed. It is huge, black and erect, an imitation male organ attached to the naked victim, that waves rigidly as he is jolted and bumped in the back of the trailer. It draws howls of ridicule and encouragement from the men behind us.

"Ahaaaa, ya fat bollocks!" somebody shrieks.

Again the cars whizz by, young fellows hanging from the windows, and I see the fake penis, erect and improbably huge, but nonetheless alarming. I finish my drink in a hurry, not knowing where to look or how to react in front of Sam.

"Why do they do that?" I ask, unable to conceal my horror, not just at the sight of this huge member, but at the mad screams of the men behind us, as if they are at the very edges of restraint, their hysterical jollity and that strange baying which reminds me of how hounds sound when on the scent of the fox. Sam shrugs his shoulders, hands gripping his thighs.

"It's just something they do in these parts. They don't know any better," he grumbles in an attempt to soothe me.

Chapter Seven

—⚅—

From the moment Sam snapped his sketchbook closed I knew he was odd and this was confirmed by the way he talked. Oddness is a word used by most people to describe behaviour which does not conform to what is considered sociable or civil. It's the opposite of that limp little word "nice" which, according to Jane Austen, means that one is civil and smiles a lot. For that reason oddness doesn't bother me. I'm quite odd myself. Although Rose never really warmed to Sam and Kate had reservations about his being too cautious for me, his oddness appealed from the beginning. The oddness was always there and I liked it. I continued to like it even when he was with that woman. She did her best to reform him, had all the orderliness of the French and went to a lot of trouble organising his life. I mustn't think of her. Of all that. That is for the therapist to hear.

Perhaps in time, if things work out the way Sam thinks they are going to, I'll be able to admire his buildings once again. They are everywhere in the city. Sam's erections. I chortle quietly thinking about Sam's erections. Never quite what he would have wanted, never sensational enough to satisfy his own imagination. That I was satisfied seems not to have mattered. Poor Sam.

I find an empty bench. Most of the workers are heading

back to their offices. The trees are heavy with colour and late summer blossom, it's a day for bees and flies and copulations of all sorts. Bare-armed girls lie around in sweetheart neckline T-shirts, their legs tanned from exposure to the summer sunshine. All marketable. Saleable. Imminently desired by the young accountant types who still jostle one another, the vestiges of schoolboy gaucheness showing in their movements.

Sam thinks big. He is less frustrated today than he was five years ago. Today there is some slight hope of his buildings in glass and steel rising from decaying riverside sites. Now that he's got the first one up, now that it's laden with awards and accolades, now that it's been scrutinised by *The Irish Times*'s environmental correspondent, he's home and dry. Sam is an idealist. That possibly explains why he left me. Nothing less than perfection. When pushed to consider the direction of his life, nothing less than perfection will do. What influences him is the delusion that I am significantly wanting, and this allows his self-deception a completeness even he never expected. But as every woman knows (and a few men), there is always someone waiting in the wings, ready to move from understudy to centre-stage performer.

Coming from the east side of the city it is impossible to avoid Sam's buildings, even if I wanted to. All those new estates which are politely termed "developments" were designed by Sam. He has finally copped on to the appeal of larger kitchens and has created these by cropping off the rear sitting-rooms in his houses. Everything in his work is dictated by budgetary restrictions, with the exception of the Cragg-Mortimer Centre, his latest and best development. Years ago he attempted to incorporate tiny additions, hints of the baroque, to the exteriors of small houses. Hints. One small, ornamented protrusion above a doorway, or on each side of the windows, hardly constitutes baroque, but the intention was there. He tired of it after a time, when he saw the outlandish colours which people chose to festoon any extra moulding on the exterior.

His architraves are distinctive. He hates Georgian architecture in any form, authentic or neo-. Boring, mindless and myopic are words he used in that connection, to the horror of a few good citizens from Edinburgh with whom we slipped into conversation once on a brief holiday to that city.

"So dark and oppressive," he moaned. "So Scandinavian in the dourest sense," he groaned as we trundled up Dundas Street in a taxi. "So bloody dark-souled!" he spat as we strolled down the Royal Mile.

"This is the oldest part of the city, my love," I informed him between gritted teeth, "older than Georgian or Regency, so stop talking through your lovely backside and give it a rest!"

Those were the early days; lusty days, full of probing and exploration. But as far as Sam is concerned, there's no escape from the Georgian fiends. Even on our honeymoon they pursued us. There we were, stretched out, having a postprandial snooze on the lawns of an old hotel in County Waterford, when they descended. The Georgian Society of Ireland. Down to examine a couple of facades that had been added to the building two centuries previously. Their leader searched madly for the toilets and asked Sam for directions. He shrugged his shoulders unhelpfully and growled something about *No comprende* to the fellow who stood before us, armed with maps and booklets. They finally decided to have a tinkle beneath the trees.

"Ladies to the elms, men to the beeches!" the man ordered resourcefully.

Somewhere in Sam's mind there is a crystal palace, locked from sight. It is very beautiful but fragile. He was ecstatic about the new entrance to the Louvre and used to scrutinise every glass dome, tower and tunnel he came upon when we travelled abroad. Once we fell into the company of a Swedish architect in Malmo who was going north in roughly the same direction as that laid out in our holiday itinerary and, over a period of days as we visited the fjords and forests, showed us some of the finest modern examples of how glass and steel cladding could be utilised in a sub-Arctic environment. Sam would have loved to build like that but instead he has mostly made decent houses for decent people, the kind of houses which will be battered by living, with the distinctive smells of each family.

Every house has its own peculiar smell. The majority of these are unexceptional smells, homey and average like the people who cause them. There are three categories of domestic odour. The first I like because I have occasionally created it myself, hankering for the security it suggests. You enter some people's homes and are immediately heartened by the smell of baking. You know for certain that there are scones, tea-cakes and perhaps even a loaf of brown bread somewhere in the kitchen. Such homes are not too tidy. You can live in them comfortably. Newspapers are strewn in the sitting-rooms, there are books piled here and there and possibly dog-hair on the carpets; and the loo-seat will be either loose or completely broken. Clean, comfortable but not especially intimidating. A sanctuary.

The other categories of homes with their characteristic smells I dislike. One thing they have in common is coldness. Irish people do not feel the cold. They wear thin blouses from the first of February on, convinced that spring has arrived. Their heads are full of the legends of St Brigid and they are too ready to interpret the activities of frogs and blackbirds as signs of impending warm weather. So they leave windows open and start to spring-clean. Cold, tidy houses are an abomination. Rose keeps a chilly place, though I lay the blame for that with Erkus. At dinner-parties at their house Erkus starts to do the washing-up between the main course and the dessert. He abandons ship completely because he's so obsessed with order. Rose is a vile cook, however, like many of those whose houses are superclean. They unnerve me with their crocheted placemats and embroidered cushions, their pristine antimacassars and fringed lampshades, these made at evening classes between courses in how to upholster furniture and conquer the art of macramé. Domestic Minervas whose talents in craft often lie unrecognised, the heart and soul of the rugby club night-out, the jolly stalwarts who provide limp sandwiches and bland-tasting canapes for the golf-club do. Great girls. Meanwhile you compliment the cook on her coffee and walnut cake but shiver beside a two-sod fire. In typically cold houses there's a lot of talk about fresh air. That means that they freshen the entire home by opening doors and windows in winter when the north wind is scything down the country. Fresh air puts iron in the soul.

The second type of cold home belongs to arty types. They too are notorious for running chilly establishments. This is because artists are usually poor. These houses smell of joss-sticks and oriental spices. Their kitchens are oniony and garlicky, which is very pleasant, because they enjoy the experimentation with foreign cuisine. Their floors are bare, wooden, varnished affairs with cotton mats thrown here and there. The curtains are thin and summery and again there's a preference for open windows from February to November.

Sam and I liked roaring fires. Every night the huge brick fireplace which rises through the centre of the sitting-room blazed and glowed, its canopy flickering in the light of the rising heat. I wonder if your woman made any attempts to alter his habits in that regard. The French can be frugal, something to do with the war and hardship. I remember reading a magazine survey of French frugality and hygiene habits which revealed that in the days when women wore roll-ons to hold their stomachs and bottoms in, the average Frenchwoman only washed hers every five years.

Rose and I get along well nowadays. We have grown accommodating towards one another, the age difference between us no longer the vast ocean of experience which once separated us. These days we chat on the phone and I can tell her anything. She and Erkus live on the south side. Where else? The estate agents call theirs a *bijou* home. That means it's a small, three-roomed cottage with a bathroom extension, a low roof, a long garden which they can scarcely manage but in which Rose grows magnificent orange poppies every summer, the address is correct and reflects all they could wish for.

The glass and steel building which Sam half-admires is on the corner of South King Street and St Stephen's Green. He told me of his grudging regard for it when I met him for coffee last week. It filled an awkward gap in the conversation, after I had mentioned the name of a good solicitor and Sam quite typically changed the subject. I know what Sam would like to create: a glass home, many-roomed, all slanting light and purity. He would like to be surrounded by the hard boniness of crystal and lead, to occupy the graceful transparencies of such a dwelling. That is part of Sam's problem. He was never happy with block walls, with facts presented as blank, ungiving obstacles.

Chapter Eight

—◊—

The green-fronted pizza parlour at the top of the street doesn't look too busy.

The sun has gone in and I want to sit. To the left are narrow tables which take two people on each side. To the right three or four smaller ones for people on their own, or for twosomes. Mathematical correctness. A waitress briskly informs me that it's a self-service salad bar as well.

"Lashings of coleslaw," the menu announces. "A simmering bed of mushrooms, garlic and real Mozzarella cheese!" it exclaims. Why they can't simply call it an excellent pizza is beyond me.

"Do you make a good pizza?" I ask the waitress. She looks at me impatiently. The question has thrown her.

"Yeah, very good," she says, scratching her head absently. "It's just that some places have too much crust and not enough cheese, and other places have crust as thin as a penny and too much tomato paste..." My voice peters out.

"Oh, it's not too thick or too thin here, just right, I'll tell the chef to give you the special, just in case," she says more confidently.

"Okay, so plenty of cheese, black olives, anchovies and garlic," I add in a burst of decisiveness.

"What would you like to drink?" she asks without looking up from her pad.

"What've you got?"

"It's there on the menu." She points carelessly with her pencil to the newspaper-sized, plastic menu. Should I have wine, to loosen up a bit, or would it depress me?

"Do you have decaff?"

Again she looks quizzically at me, as if I'm some kind of looper.

"Decaffeinated coffee," I explain patiently.

"No. Tea, coffee, minerals, milk, water. That's it," she says brusquely.

"Cidona so."

"We don't do that."

"Rock shandy."

She puts down her pad and regards me as if I'm having her on.

"Okay. Orange-juice then, whatever..." I say, then change my mind again, remembering I don't like orange-juice. "Sorry. Scrub that." I smile to placate her, hoping she'll see the funny side. Her expression is deadpan.

"Just make it water," I say humbly.

"Water," she replies, pursing her lips. "You're sure about that now?" she adds, before turning on her heel. Waitresses can be formidable when they choose.

Thinking about Kate, Rose and Daniel, or Aunt Florrie and Uncle Theo, everybody from years ago, I realise that I've been cast off by life. I am a superfluous extra part that has evolved to the limits of its potential and must now be left to live out its time. Sam cannot allow himself to consider that. Especially now. He never entertained such thoughts at any time in the past, if I remember correctly.

At the next table a young couple fuss over their child. It looks about a year and a half. They look about twenty. When they're my age, their child will be a teenager with the capacity to reproduce itself. At one time I assumed that everything just went on and on, that every generation had a new chance, a second go at optimism. But that is a common mistake. There is no second chance for some people. You live and you die and nothing that has made you happy, no enthusiasm, achievement or pleasure will matter one iota once you die because there's nobody to respond to the signal, nobody to pass on or add to what has been achieved. This feeling crushes in on me and I struggle for composure. I'm in Happyland after all, the place where the young in one another's arms carry on for ever and ever and ever.

Maybe I didn't want children that deeply. Maybe if I'd really wanted them, I'd have succeeded in persuading him to go to the clinic. That's what Kate suggested once. I can scarcely forgive her that, even though she's dead now. I might have thought so myself — I occasionally still do — but I know in my heart that that's a punishing thought which people in my position should have no dealing with. *They brought it on themselves. It's a punishment. Her jeans (genes) are too tight. No lead in his pencil. Too selfish. Too career-minded. Didn't really want children or else something would have happened by now.* We've been through the mill of received wisdom, Sam and I. In that we are still one. That Kenyan woman who was stoned for being barren, according to the *Guardian* article, almost had her brains smashed in for something that was beyond her control. And what about her man, her master, her husband? Some men never even consider that it can happen to them. Who knows what the real situation was? The awful point is that it was she, the Kenyan woman, who bore the evidence of some dread, internal drought, it was she whose belly never swelled.

My pizza has arrived. It is exactly as ordered, piled with

52

shining olives, slivers of anchovy, succulent with tomato and thick, soft cheese.

"Is that all right?" a voice demands. The waitress's eyes are not unkind, despite the cut of her voice. She obviously thinks I've been let out from somewhere for the afternoon.

"Just perfect," I answer.

The first bite is a mixture of contrasts, the crust firm and crisp-edged, the filling deep, with sweet and salty flavours. When all else fails, I can still enjoy eating. I call her back and order a half-bottle of the house red, which she fetches wordlessly. I can think when I eat and drink. Some of my best thinking is done on a Saturday morning, when the week's work is finished, and things can be approached at leisure. Meals are important for the time they allow to ponder and consider.

During the years that we tried and tried, Sam kept busy. While I was tripping in and out of the clinic and taking the pills, while we went in for a great deal of hectic sex at certain times and none at all at others (everybody telling us to relax and it will just happen) Sam worked. I was busy too but somehow my mind was drawn down. There were times when I was like a kite, depending on wind to lift me high with hope, alert to any optimism, anything that would do the trick.

The initial tests were basic and undaunting. But months pass and they increase in complexity. You are tunnelled into. You feel guilty. You are inept in some vital way. The clinic is a modern redbrick place, approached by a discreet back entrance, which deals with pregnant women as well as the pariahs of failed womanhood. There are leafy sycamores outside the professor's rooms. Each time you go, he asks if there is any news, his foxy blue eyes hopping between your face and the report sheet in front of him. There is never any news. He is always optimistic, talks cheerily about the possibilities of multiple pregnancies. I do not want a multiple pregnancy. I am not a rabbit. So they poke and investigate, inject me inside and out, turn a machine on my stomach and get a picture of that little fist of a womb. I am so delighted to see it, having grown convinced that I have none. Afterwards I rush out and buy two dresses and a pair of shoes. Even to see my own womb tells me something.

During the dye test they discuss the Falklands War but I am excluded from that discussion because a green sheet divides my top half from my bottom half; my thinking, living self from the apparently intricate but stubbornly inanimate part that they are probing. What I think in my top half does not seem to matter. They have work to do and must be objective. There is no connection between the two halves.

Sam seems sympathetic. Each time a series of tests is concluded, he becomes more helpful than ever, more solicitous, knowing I'm about to tell him that the prof sees no point in going any further with my tests until he has his done.

"Won't you go?" I beg him. He doesn't answer. The matter is up to me entirely. He never cracks. Every so often my anger builds up like a huge watery sac that must explode. I think of alternatives. If I wanted to, I could make trouble. The marriage could be dissolved. I could argue non-consummation if I wanted to, though that's the farthest thing from the truth. The point is I don't want to leave Sam on account of this: it's a nothing in the overall scheme of things but he makes it into a something by refusing to have the test.

I didn't think he'd leave me. Goes to show. Some people will always follow the easy option. The admiring, soothing one. Some people, most of us, will bear with the companion who affirms, who builds us up, who doesn't remind us of our innumerable failings. I never saw it as a failing but my presence was enough.

54

The wine is palatable and I lay into it with gusto. I have three hours to spare before returning to Dr Flynn-Mitchell. Something has gone very wrong. The plans for my life were drawn up on a rough basis, much as the draughtsmen at Sam's office tinker around with proposals. Some are basic sketches, others are fully explored, whole projections for future events. I had plans too. I had projected a future, had every reason to expect the whirl of a noisy household. So had Sam. But something has gone horribly wrong. I ponder the statistics. The official ones vary from one in ten couples to one in six. Could it be something more significant, I wonder, my attention caught by some framed pictures on the wall of the pizza-place. The usual images, an offshoot of Warhol fever. Restaurants actually mount advertisements. The cover page of a *New Yorker* is framed in shiny red. Beside it an advertisement for a Japanese sound-system. There are smart quips in abundance. Beside me a picture of a panda. It asks you to support the struggle against deforestation and shows the sooty-eyed bear munching on eucalyptus. The message is clear, the image mounted matter-of-factly between those for the *New Yorker* and the Japanese stereo-system. These are today's issues: art, money, environment.

The panda-bear is on the way out unless we stop razing the forests of Southeast Asia. The list of endangered species is a mile long — birds, reptiles, fish and mammals from the Arctic to Antarctica — along the coasts and up rivers, on mountains, hills, in forests, wherever the violent human mammal has set foot.

But suppose the whole thing is winding down for us too? Suppose there's a planned obsolescence built in to the species? Suppose Sam is merely one of the catalysts, that he and I are the beginning of the end of the tribe? Despite what happened with that woman. Of course we would have to be different. Life can be so perverse. Either I've been wildly happy, ecstatically so, or I've been in the doldrums. Either I've felt full of courage, ready to risk life and limb, or else I've been petrified, a quaking mouse beneath my physical largeness.

Sam is big too. He grew from a thickset boy into a big, square-shouldered and brown-haired man. Daniel and Kate and Rose always found him cross-grained, that bit diffident and awkward. When Aunt Florrie met him, she didn't know what to make of him because he showed not the slightest interest in her and didn't respond to her jokes. He made an effort all right, the corner of his lips nicked upwards in slight humour, but later on she said that it was obvious to her that Sam Wright lived on another planet. Sam was always a bit of a mystery to the Troys, the Bardons and the Binchys. No matter. They do not dictate everything.

Getting him to accompany me to fashion shoots and first-nights even when he had time became an effort after a few months. Dragging him would be more like it. As my reputation as a photographer has grown more secure, so too has his discomfort with flamboyant types, with attention-seekers and chatterboxes. He would come every so often yet, despite introductions, seemed to step back, to withdraw, while I roved and scavenged for photographs. What others thought in that regard has never concerned me because I too hold myself at a remove from the circus of the theatre and fashion worlds, although of course a certain compromise is necessary. People are hungry for any kind of attention, occasionally nab you on the pretence of having a chat but privately hope you'll rig up the camera tout de suite. But they are my bread and butter, such people. Old rhinoceros actresses, their horns nicked by one bad review too many; effete actors, all gush and herd-instinct. Glass people who shield themselves from too much light, from real walls in real homes, preferring the fragile props designed by set artistes, the tawny manipulation of lighting schemes, the selectivity of my lenses.

Chapter Nine

—m—

Our kitchen is square and low-ceilinged, with dark stained beams from which we hang dried flowers, pots and pans. They accumulate grease and dust because I forget all about them. The kitchen is not as original as we like to think but the saving grace is that the place is lived in, with the dog's basket beneath a cut-out portion of the cupboards and a smaller one in the corner for an old tomcat which visits infrequently to recover from his war wounds.

I am least certain of Sam in the company of others. I insist on eating there, though he has other ideas. It is my way of saying that I will not be coerced into adopting the harsh social formalities of our generation.

But some Friday nights we have visitors, friends, acquaintances whose company we enjoy variously.

"Let's eat inside," Sam says, nodding towards the dining room.

"It's nicer here."

"I know it's nice, but it's not, well...the other place is better."

Such are our little tussles. Harmless, inconsequential matters.

"Don't be so hung-up on formalities!" I say. He bristles. I watch his shoulders stiffen despite the smile. Then he calls me an inverted snob. I am indignant, the more so because there's a grain of truth in what he says. I am also anxious that Sam and I be liked, that we fit in. We are just like most other people of our age, class and educational background. But another tide sweeps around us. There are currents and undertows which tear at the simplest costuming of our lives, telling us again that we are not the same.

"Maybe you are right," I say. "Maybe we'll eat inside."

He relents then. "It's okay, we'll stay here if that's what you want."

But I am flustered. It doesn't take much now. I never know what's the right thing to do. Uncertainties complicate the simplest tasks.

"I hate bourgeois carry-on, the new kind," I mutter.

"Well, we'll stay in here if that's what you really want!" he says, catching my wrist and pulling me towards him, nuzzling my earlobe. "We're all bourgeois anyway — yuppies, dinkies, wrinklies; you name the acronym and it's bourgeois."

I kiss him suddenly and his lips part, his mouth the sweetest anybody could ever taste.

"I suppose you're right. It's just that I hate those stuffed shirts we all grew up with, who think it's neat to have obnoxious dinner-parties and discuss writers and artists whose work they just skim through at Christmas or in museums on summer holidays."

"Bullshit artists," says Sam.

"Shitheads. Our life is full of them."

"Does that make us ditto?" he asks, kissing me back then, his hand pulling my blouse out from my skirt, moving swiftly up towards my breasts.

"Heaven forbid! Who cares? Just carry on!"

By the time we're finished, we have to rush everything. I spread the pink and green tablecloth we bought in a desert village in Tunisia. I like the kitchen because this is where I work with hot colour, where I grow enthusiastic about cooking, about watching people enjoy the food we serve. There are mental images to be stored which the camera can rarely capture and, even when it does, makes an artifice of them.

Wet, greasy lips, the quiet way Sam eats – tidily, contained but with concentration. Rose eats with unrestrained gusto and makes a feast of breakfast time, with huge sugared bowls of cereal dolloped with cream. Our father is busy conserving his colon and drinks bran mixed with water. Evening food is more my line, when I can use the most succulent herbs from the kitchen garden beyond the window, and chop basil and thyme with abandon. Real cooks, true gastronomes, are more restrained in their use of herbs.

"Do you think I try too hard to please other people?" I ask Sam. The cranium scraping is underway yet again. These days I am as bare as mussel flesh. Sam doesn't answer immediately, he is absorbed in wiping down a couple of bottles of red wine. "You don't actually try to please," he grunts, uncorking a bottle, "but you worry too much about what they think."

This is Sam being sensible. Sam the realist, Sam the reasonable man. I burst out laughing and he doesn't see why. I can't even explain it to him. The subject is closed. He will discuss some things only in terms of me, never with regard to himself. And some part of me hardens each time I watch him carry on as if he had nothing whatsoever to do with the situation. It is even worse whenever I consider the way everything in existence seems preoccupied with multiplication and continuity – with growing, blossoming, fucking, blooming and bursting its pod.

There's a knock at the front door. It's too late to pursue

the matter, and Sam goes to let them in. Tony and Sandrine work with him. Tony is his partner and Sandrine is the new draughtswoman. We wonder what their relationship is, presume a romantic complicity but are never quite sure. We have hardly closed the door when Anna and Mark arrive and there is a confused round of greetings in the hallway. We have known Anna and Mark since college days. Both of them hovered at a distance the first time I had coffee with Sam in the canteen. I was in First Arts and he was well through his architecture course. We talked about home and people we knew, and he asked after Rose, whom people always enquired about because her reputation for being a wild woman had grown enormously in the course of a few years. Universities seethe with seedling relationships such as ours was.

Anna and Mark met when she was in Third Arts and he had just failed his finals in commerce. He made no attempt to do re-sits but went straight out and found a part-time reporting job with one of the evening rags. Now he writes a sports column called "On Your Marks," hosts a television programme and covers international rugby for radio. He is amusing company, if a little dense at times: easy-going, smoothskinned, bursting with good health. Years ago, Anna wanted to become an interpreter. Now she translates German business documents at home, technical stuff which doesn't interest her but keeps her in touch with the language. Their four children are noisy, sociable and spoiled. I have not lost all sense of proportion. Even with things the way they are, there are children I identify immediately as either adorable or tiresome. Mark and Anna's fall into the latter category. I have never been so anxious for motherhood that I could want any child.

Tony is devoid of pretence and tells the most outrageously antisocial jokes. Humour is another thing that the arbiters of liberal good taste have dispensed with. Women are not supposed to enjoy anti-feminist jokes, we are all (men and women both) supposed to be appalled at racist gags and to abhor gay, lesbian, incest and sex jokes, being too aware of ourselves, too well-read in psychological trends to admit to enjoying such things.

Sam takes Sandrine's jacket. She is demure and mannerly. He has assured me beforehand that I will take to her. The fact that he likes her at all fascinates me. He is by no means a man who flares brilliantly in company — wit and conversational verve scorching the air are quite alien to him. It is all I can do to get him to go out. Or to visit Daniel and Kate. Or to tolerate Rose or, worse still, Erkus. Erkus-Jerkus, Sam calls him. He likes Sandrine and accepts Tony much as one accepts one's own skin. Tony has always been around. They met in college, two boys from opposite ends of the country, Tony having come straight from a huge diocesan college, Sam from the grey-walled grammar school outside Clonfoy. The practice has been in operation for ten years and together they've hatched a few successful plans, along with the occasional disaster.

I rarely inflict Sam on my friends. He is uncomfortable with bookish types or artists. "Bluffer!" he'll spit when I tell him that so-and-so has just brought out a new novel. "Another slim volume no doubt," he drolls, convinced that most writers are hell-bent on conning the public into thinking that they're geniuses. Ergo, the smaller the book, the slimmer the collection of poetry, the more esoteric and brilliant the work. Sam has never written. He sees the world in pictures, paints in lines and perspectives, in precisely calculated quantities, apprehends the world on the basis of stone and steel and glass. He has no inkling of the mind-teasing hungers, the chance little nugget of a word, the half-formed idea, that drive writers day after day. In my line of work I meet them all, the deluded, the preeners, but also the very talented. These last are certainly never found in a newsroom, where scarcely literate sub-editors caption my photographs inanely or reduce them to one-eighth of the original size. Because Sam is top dog along with Tony, he has scant notion of compromise.

Sandrine is well back in an armchair, her legs crossed; Tony and Sam are on the sofa; Mark and Anna sit on either side of me. I direct my conversation lightly towards Sandrine. She looks pleasant. Her hair is straight light brown, almost blonde but not quite, and worn combed carelessly to one side. She is as slim as a whippet, yet no fashion-doll. Her clothes make few concessions to modernity: she wears a loose mauve skirt, a white blouse and pink shoes. All I know of her is what Sam has told me, that she left her husband behind in France, took herself off with a few belongings and little money and eventually made her way to Ireland.

The evenings are lengthening once again and the late sun slants in behind Tony, Sam and Sandrine, lighting their heads and shoulders. Our voices are still soft, because Sandrine is the relative newcomer and as a group we have not fully loosened up. Outside, a blackbird's whistle whorls the air, cars drone in the distance on the other side of the high wall at the far end of the garden, a plane takes off over the city. I am conscious of a shift, a change in the way we view one another. It is a minuscule thread of a feeling, nothing more.

"Ah, you have this crystal!" she exclaims, springing up to cross the room and admire Sam's leaded glass collection.

"Sam's circus," I say benignly. This is one of his indulgences. A collection of tiny animals and birds, Czechoslovakian lead crystal pieces, which catch the light and refract a world of prisms. Every year he adds more pieces. They are naive forms. Little bears, prickly hedgehogs, spiders, birds, flowers, dogs and artful cats that glitter like crushed gemstones in the evening light as Sandrine approaches.

"So beautiful," she sighs, lifting one gently. Her hands are slim and brown. I am transfixed by her accent, the light, lisping voice, her inability to master the "bew" part of "beautiful."

"Yes, beautiful," I say, unconsciously correcting her. My voice sounds crass and ordinary.

"You have good taste," she tells Sam. He nods in acknowledgement, conceals his pleasure.

"Have you lived here long?" I ask, knowing the answer.

"Six months."

"Do you like it?"

"*Very* much," she says with conviction. "People are extremely sympathetic to me."

Anna swirls the ice in her glass distractedly, her face turned towards Sandrine, her eyes nonetheless absorbed by some private concern.

"Let's eat anyway," I say. "You must be starving—you like to cook?"

Sandrine throws her head back and laughs heartily. "Not in the least. You think that because I am French I like to cook?"

"Probably," I admit.

"I 'ate cooking but I love eating what others cook!" she says effusively, then gasps and exclaims in puffs of pleasure when we enter the kitchen. Sam and I exchange looks. It seems to me that Sandrine is someone who can be pleased. My love of cooking is inherited from Kate. She was no whizz with ambitious stuff but her enthusiasm always showed. I adore the smells, the colours, textures and arrangements that go with eating. My repertoire is limited. I've never attended courses that some people pay vast sums of money for. I don't go in for copper saucepans and the kitchen isn't a technical sanctuary filled with gadgets. Sauces are my speciality. I have a confident, generous hand, which is useful now that Sam has entered his vegetarian phase, and have prepared two courses for this meal: peppers stuffed with beef, olives, Parmesan cheese, nutmegs, onion for the carnivores among us, nut roast for those of the other persuasion. Sam and Sandrine go for the nut roast.

"Are you one too?" says Anna, splitting her pepper in two.

"One what?" says Sandrine vaguely. "Oh, vegetarian — yes."

"This is like a truth session. Let's all confess our secret predilections!" Mark says.

"At least you've company, Sam," says Tony. "How d'ye put up with him, Hanna, cookin' two kinds of meals, wha'?"

Vegetarianism is not a problem. It is how we are meant to be, according to the latest theories. The fact that I can't turn away from a rare sliver of beef, a tender piece of lamb, juicy quails and fleshy lobster, is my problem. I err on the side of both ignorance and greed. I am not convinced that Sam really likes vegetarian fare as much as he claims. It is a recent development. Apart from his dreams of glass, barrel-vaulted mansions and his preoccupation with lead crystal, he has recently joined Greenpeace, Save the Whale, the Vegetarian Society and Chickens' Lib. Even I do not know everything that goes on in his head. This sudden interest in the preservation of the planet is disturbing. It is not normal. Even though I am ready to extend the boundaries of what is termed normality at the drop of the proverbial hat, Sam's sudden turn to vegetarianism is not normal. That is to say, it masks something else.

Chapter Ten

—☓—

Every Easter the whole family gets together. That is, Kate's family, the Bardons, and all their married attachments. We join the aunts and uncles and cousins and head off to the hills for the day. There's a great deal of fuss and bother in the preparations but despite all the minor irritations everyone usually agrees that it was a great day. Daniel is an unknown quantity to Kate's lot. Her being the second wife had them on their guard for a while but they got over their suspicion. They're all go and activity, unused to someone who sits with a book on his lap, smoking a pipe. For that reason they imagine him to be very calm, and when Kate gives out to him either Joachim or Theo tells her to leave that good man alone. That annoys her. She feels they interfere sometimes when they should not, that they take the man's side no matter what.

Theo is a teacher. He has worked in Germany, in Ttibingen and Heidelberg. He had a German girlfriend years back, before the war, prior to marrying Aunt Dot and adopting a son called Bill. He has always admired the German way of celebrating Easter. Every year we children are given hard-boiled unshelled eggs to paint. This more than makes up for the leaden seriousness of Good Friday when we have to sit through long services in the big cathedral above the town. The priests come out in two rows on the altar, then we stand for what seems like ages while the gospel is chanted and the Boy Scouts do their best to make music with bugles. But on Easter Sunday there are the eggs and the knowledge that the adults will have secreted smaller chocolate eggs in our Easter baskets the previous night. Theo tries his hand at making ginger-flavoured Easter hare biscuits. They usually taste too gingery, not sweet enough, but we like the idea of them. He has other ideas too—he gathers hazel branches for Aunt Dot. They decorate their sitting-room with these. Aunt Florrie thinks it's a lot of nonsense, but the yellow catkins are pretty. They droop delicately and we're allowed to decorate the branches with small ornaments, bits of coloured paper, sweets tied to pieces of bright thread.

One of the women takes responsibility for the lamb, another for the turkey. These are roasted late on Saturday night so as to be cold for the next day's picnic. My mother prefers baking bread to any other form of cookery. She swears like mad during the preparation of large meals at festive occasions and is happier dealing with smaller culinary feats.

The next day we set out, the Bardons (Aunt Florence's family in their two white cars), the Binchys, and us, the Troys. There are five cars on the way to Rock Bog and we've taken the precaution of packing rain gear. Aunt Florrie has brought a tent in case of a downpour, though how we'll all fit inside is a question she seems not to have considered. The women are dressed practically, with the exception of Florrie. On her head perches a large straw hat, heavy with fruit and flowers, woven together with a navy ribbon. Her dress is navy and white, with a loose bow at the neck. Kate is in trousers and stout walking-shoes, with a red polo-neck sweater and a hacking-jacket. Joachim's wife, Lizzie, is her usual self: she wears huge goggle-eyed spectacles, her hair is unwashed and she smells stale but as ever has brought bags of Maltesers for all the children. These can be purchased only across the border in the North and therefore all the more valued. We like her because of her odd ways. Birthday parties in their house are not popular because she cannot cook. On the other hand, birthdays at Aunt Florrie's can be tense affairs. The food is considered good but once it is eaten we have to be careful about where we go, and most places are out of bounds.

At Rock Bog we don't do much except eat and walk around for a few hours. The big problem is finding a suitable spot for the picnic. Mostly we opt for a sheltered copse within a mile of the top of the mountain. The cars drone slowly and heavily as they climb up the winding road. My ears pop as we ascend.

"That's what it's like on a plane," says Rose, who has flown to France on a school exchange. If I swallow, the popping sensation goes, but I have to stick at it. One of the cars behind has stopped and Aunt Florrie hops out with a bowl in her hand, her face cross. Her son Jamie has been car-sick again. Rose and I laugh, wondering whom he sprayed. Jamie is known to hold on until it's too late and spew the contents of his stomach all over the place.

Finally we arrive. There are cloths to be spread, big white squares, then plates and cutlery, unbreakable glasses and mugs to be placed. The air is chill, even though it's well into April, and everybody except Florrie has some sort of jacket or shawl to keep warm. Jamie looks withdrawn.

"What happened?" I ask him.

"Got sick."

"I know, I know, but where?" I am eager for details, the gorier the better.

"On the baby."

Delighted, I head off to tell Rose. Already the cousins are forming into groups: some have begun to play games; others just hover near the food. The men's voices sound deep and gruff; I can't make out what they're saying but their presence is strong, smells of aftershave, smells of smoke. My father has lit up and a blue stream of smoke is quickly whipped away by the light wind. Everything is pushing up from the earth. There are white flowers in clumps on the top layer of the bog, and the birches are like a shimmering screen between us and the spring sun. We settle within the doubtful shelter of mountain ash which hasn't yet bloomed, ravenous.

As it turns out, the turkey, which Kate cooked most years, is a great success. She's relieved, having always felt herself to be less competent in domestic matters than most other women. My father and she exchange looks. Even Rose laughs. Aunt Florrie has cooked the lamb and fusses because there isn't enough rosemary through it.

"It's lovely, dear," says her husband. Henry is a quiet, dapper man, with a narrow moustache. Nobody has ever fathomed what he really thinks about, and he spend his time driving between the five garages he owns in two counties and also (though this is less spoken of) taking things in from the North as favours for people. Sometimes he gives the impression of being overpowered by Florrie but the truth is that he's the only person who can deal with her and calm her down.

As happens every year, someone brings a camera and a photograph is taken, establishing babies once and for all in the family circle, recording changes in the women and developing firmness in the men. That Easter Sunday in the early sixties Kate murmurs, "*Go mbeirimíd go léir beo ar an am seo arís*", may we all be alive this time next year, and everybody repeats the words eagerly. Then Uncle Theo takes the photograph during the dessert. I like photographs, regardless of how I feel, and that particular day sense the sheer force of being alive. Then with a bowl of trifle in my lap and a spoon halfway to my mouth as the camera clicks, I can take it for granted that I'm loved.

Chapter Eleven

—⚹—

The conversation is lively. We laugh a lot, though Sam is withdrawn. Sandrine seems to be enjoying herself. Her demureness holds my attention. Mark and Tony argue fiercely about the Triple Crown and the ins and outs of French-style rugby.

"Give me Aussie football any day," says Anna, helping herself to more wine. "Noice toight little shorts and plenty of shoulder muscle!" We laugh as she mimics the Australian accent. "Does the Sheilas a power of good, the old Australian rules does," says Mark.

"Which reminds me," Tony interrupts, "how do Australian women show their men they're glad to see them?"

"How?" asks Sandrine, voice quivering with good humour. Sam clears his throat pointedly. He does this when he is less than comfortable with what is being said. Tony has noticed his censoriousness.

They put their knees behind their ears and — "

"Okay-okay-okay," Sam says nervously. Anna and I look at one another, Mark and Tony roar with laughter. Sandrine smiles. Tony decides not to go on with the joke and grimaces in an apologetic way at her.

"It's all right, I'm not shocked," she says pleasantly.

"Course not, Frenchie, it's us that are shocked," says Mark in mock-serious tones.

Anna asks Sandrine about her life in France. She is separated.

Her husband lives in Fontainebleau and breeds Dalmatians. Sandrine tells her that they had no children. "Fortunately," she scowls, " —and you?"

"Nearly half a team," says Mark jocosely.

"Four," says Anna.

Sandrine rolls her eyes in disbelief and lets out a subdued whistle. "That is a lot of work, I think?"

"Ah, but we had fun makin' it!" Mark interrupts again.

"You're right, Sandrine, it's far too much work," says Anna.

"Well, at least they're over the worst stage now," I say, gauging that the youngest must be at school. Anna hesitates.

"To tell you the truth, Hanna..." Her voice peters out and she looks rather helpless; then mumbles something about having something in the offing.

"Spit it out, Anna, tell them!" Mark says impatiently, face beaming like a boy who has scored the goal of the match.

We all erupt in a bawling round of congratulations. Anna is miserable. My feelings are mixed. *Hadn't she ever heard of taking precautions?* Another part of me feels sorry for her. Bang go her hopes of becoming an interpreter. Another ten years postponement more than likely, while she waits for the little sprog to grow up. Yet I blame her. Maybe she chose to be a sitting duck, getting pregnant time and again. Maybe she's just lazy. There's no excuse for it nowadays, not if you really want to avoid getting pregnant. In an instant I hear myself level the easy, dismissive terms at someone who has never done me any harm, whom I quite like. The easy judgements circle in my head, I too can point a finger, just like those people in Kenya with the woman they stoned, I too know how to condemn, stare and parcel up someone else's life. The very thing I abhor.

72

The two men are too busy backslapping even to notice Anna. Even Sam joins in, rocking back and forth in his chair. Mark is kingpin: the man who has got his woman pregnant, put her up the spout, with a bun in the oven. Sam is some performer. He missed his vocation. Never have I seen him so gregarious, so devil-may-care as now. He pours a brandy for Mark and insists on a toast. We all join in. By now I have recovered my equilibrium.

"You'll be fine," I assure Anna. I want her to know that whatever happens she'll be all right. I will approve of her no matter what. She has done nothing to be disapproved of anyway.

When Sandrine and Tony make to leave, I suggest meeting her in town someday.

"I would like that very much," she replies. Tony helps her with her jacket. I notice her feet, how fine and dainty they are in those pink shoes. Hers is a discreet, gentle beauty.

We are mellow, neither tired nor randy when we go to bed. Sam sits down, and yanks off his socks, green ones that he wondered about wearing earlier, thinking they might be too bright. Every so often he stops and stares at the opposite wall. I undress quickly. Neither of us will make overtures. In the bathroom I remove make-up, wash my teeth, pick absently at some congealed soap in the soap-dish. After washing my face I hold the towel close. Deeply puzzled. Confused. I wish Kate was here. But there's no point phoning at this hour. What can I say that would make sense?

As I stomp back into the bedroom, Sam jerks his head quizzically. I mumble something about hurrying up. He doesn't reply. I am mortally offended, indignant. So is he but he can't admit it. We hurt because Anna is pregnant and I am not; we are galled by it, as if someone viciously lashed at an open wound and doused it with acid.

"Sam," I say, not looking at him. He doesn't turn away. What is it about me that this man refuses to talk? Do I hound him? Must he retreat into caves of silence every time?

"What?" he says eventually, as if I've just asked the time.

"I can't do any more."

"I know that. It's all right," he says softly.

"That's not what I meant."

He uses this tactic every single time. I throw myself on the bed. We took trouble with this bedroom. It is warm and comforting, as a bedroom should be. The walls are rag-painted in pale green, the paintwork is white and the floor varnished wood with green and yellow Berber rugs. It is the place where the best part of our lives could be lived if only we could get on with it.

"Sam. Please, please see someone!"

"Don't talk nonsense," he snaps, leaving the room. You'd swear I had asked him to stand on his head naked in the middle of rush-hour traffic.

"You must!" I call, struggling to keep my temper. The bathroom door opens abruptly and he comes back in.

"There's only so much that can be done. Keep taking the tablets for another while."

"That's just typical of you! Typical of your whole family! None of you can bear the slightest thought of physical imperfection; you have to throw the blame on somebody else!"

He ignores me. I begin to scream. "Selfish pig. Let me keep taking pills for no bloody reason. They've found nothing bloody *wrong* with me!' I swipe a book off the floor and leave for the other bedroom.

It is not too much to ask that he has the test done. Or that I become pregnant like many other women my age. Time is running out. It's not as if he has scruples about wanking into a glass tube. He is not hung-up on antediluvian superstitions. But time spills away from us. Every minute lost like sand on the wind. I think back to my childhood, rake the ground of the past for some sign of what was to come. He is so blind that he does not even consider the possible side-effects of those tablets. Twins, triplets, quads and quins. Well stuff it for a business, I don't want multiples.

In biological terms I am old. In a primitive culture I would be a grandmother and I would be respected. I care about being respected. Women envy me; the housebound, those imprisoned by their children. But they also cast me out from among them. Bitter matrons. Men suspect me: barren, witch-woman, seductress. If I don't have children, that must mean I am a selfish, self-seeking, career-oriented bitch who is interested in one thing only.

It is not too much to ask. I am competent. I have passed exams all my life and succeed in almost everything I undertake. Sometimes I dream of a baby. It is soft and naked. I hold it to my bare skin. I have never held a child like that but I am sure of how it feels. There is nothing more delicious, more absolving, more hopeful than the skin of a baby. Such are my dreams.

The bedside light clicks off in the next room. A wind has blown up outside, making a strange moaning sound as it strikes the telegraph wires. What Kate used to call sí-ghaoth or fairy-music when Rose and I were children.

We face death. Not having a child forces Sam and me to look at it, eye to eye. We do not always like what we see; there is nothing between us and it. No buffer. No triviality. No light.

75

Chapter Twelve

—⁓—

The pizza-place is busy with mid-afternoon snackers, schoolgirls on the run who light cigarettes with urgency, women rapt in earnest chat who gaze into each other's eyes with the intensity of lovers. Phrases drift soft as ribbon on the air. "...and then he..." or "So I said..." or again "an' what do ya think she did then but..."

It is a more political time than most men will ever know. Things are at their most subversive when friendships are bonded by good-quality gossip, conscienceless betrayals of men's fears, secrets and peculiarities. Meanwhile, in elected assemblies the world over, in offices, on golf-courses and in squash-courts, the same thing happens under a different guise.

Friendship with Anna has been a growing disappointment. When bereft of lovers, we should have friends. Good friends. I veer between Anna and Rose, never satisfied with either. Anna has grown primmer, smugger, with the birth of every child. The protective instinct awoken by maternity has been subverted because of the endless measuring-up sessions which she has endured at the hands of others. Is she good enough as a mother? Is she calm enough, reassuring enough, selfless enough, content enough?

I am critical of her for bowing to such pressures. She, who used to be bright and rakish, full of humour and abandon, is being worn down. Phrases which would not have passed her lips years ago are now uttered with arresting regularity. God willing. God knows. If God preserves us all. She has forgotten the high points of our college days, claims not to recall how she once stood shivering in a wardrobe for two hours with no clothes on when her boyfriend's companions unexpectedly arrived back at the flat. She has forgotten the times she was a dab hand at stealing a demi-Camembert from the supermarket; she doesn't remember the library books she would drop into her loose trousers as a favour to friends less nimble-fingered. In fifteen years or less, Anna will look like a dowager from a Gilbert and Sullivan operetta. Instead of a dowager's hump across her shoulders, she'll have a mental one, fully developed, full of sanctimoniousness and censure.

Rose and I are pandas. The image on the wall. How beautiful everything in the world is, given the chance! How absolutely bewitching, how full of mystery and strength and delicacy is every living thing! I consider the forests, the eucalyptus, the bamboo, the banana trees, their leaves pounded by monsoon rains. Then I pour myself a fourth glass of wine.

Chapter Thirteen

—◇◇◇—

Rose is twenty. The house is full of visitors. It is Dan and Kate's anniversary and they have thrown a party. Dan is still leisurely and good-humoured, Kate a bright knot of activity. She has made new friends over the years, gives full vent to her nature through the art club. The house is hung with shaky watercolours. In the bedroom she and Dan share, there's one oil-painting, a self-portrait. The words "Me at Forty-Three" are scrawled on the back. It is thickly layered and clownish. I cannot understand why anyone should view themselves like that.

We have helped prepare things. Rose is sulking. In my eyes she is already grown-up, can do what she likes without asking permission. Since I cannot cook and will not learn for years to come, Rose makes trifles, cakes, and an alternative main course she has just discovered called lasagne. She pours scorn on the idea of serving up slices of cold meat and fowl. "So bourgeois!" she mutters, stabbing the meat. Some people, she says, should broaden their culinary horizons and move beyond Maura Laverty's *Full and Plenty*.

The table is heavy with food and crockery, colourful, gleaming. When I protest that it's *nice*, she turns impatiently.

"Nice! Of course it's bloody nice!" she mimics. "Isn't everything in this goddamn house nice? Isn't that all anybody wants?"

Rose has adopted an American idiom since leaving school and going to drama college. Dan and Kate put it down to her wanting to play Linda in *Death of a Salesman*.

"Well, everybody will like the lasagne," I say to pacify her. My mind is absorbed in the hope that Cousin Bill will come. He is three years older than me. I am crazy about him. Unlike most of the boys around, he's shy, to my mind cultured, and knows how to tease without mocking. He's good fun to be with, and I feel safe with him, can try a few things on him and test for reactions. He hopes to become a priest.

"Five people at the most will go for it," she answers with shocking definiteness. "You, me, Dan, Bill and maybe Florrie."

I laugh, understanding immediately that the only reason Florrie will try the lasagne is for the sake of sophistication.

"Course, the only reason you'll eat it is for fear of falling down in the eyes of Blessed Bill. Eejit!" she taunts.

"Who?" I ask, turning to busy myself with the cutlery.

"Blessed Bill and Holy Hanna." She is bent double at her own humour.

In the sitting-room Uncle Joachim plays the piano while Theo croons along. People come and go in the kitchen and Kate's face is flushed. According to Rose, they're a right crowd of fools. She stands disdainfully, hand on her hip, watching them move around one another. On occasions like this my mother's family is gruff and awkward. They come up to her and Dan and congratulate them.

"Sixteen years, a big day," says Theo's wife, shaking hands formally.

"Yez made it this far so," is Joachim's comment. "There'll be no partin' now."

I suppose not, says Dan, pouring himself a drink at the sideboard.

"But I'm thinking of doing a trade-in one of these days!" Kate quips. "As they say, you're never too old..."

The laughter drifts towards us through the double-doors and into the sitting-room. Rose is furious. These days her moods are unpredictable.

"Just listen to them, listen to *her!*" she whispers. Her eyes glitter dangerously. "What age does she think she is anyway?" She turns quickly away and lifts a photograph. It is Dan and Kate's wedding-day picture. Just as quickly she replaces it as if it were mad hot.

"Kate'd do anything for you," I tell her. What I mean is that Kate loves her more than anything, takes more care with Rose than with anybody else.

"Easy for you to say," she retorts.

The afternoon passes slowly. I have forgotten the time. The adults mingle and chat. Someone plinks intermittently on the piano. The younger people have formed a group of their own, although Rose is nowhere to be seen.

Bill has come. He is tall and dark-haired, with strong white teeth. His expression is full of quirky puzzlement. We stand awkwardly and admire the silver tray which the family have had inscribed with names and good wishes. I replace it in its hiding-place in the garage whence it will be brought later, wrapped and beribboned.

The summer has been unusually calm. Bill and I walk down the garden towards Tongs Lough. He has spent two years at university in Dublin, learning French, Italian and Philosophy. I am filled with admiration for his genius.

"I think I'll study Italian when I leave school," I tell him, eager to display my readiness for new challenges. "And Philosophy perhaps." He nods; then says that philosophy has perhaps something to do with the meaning of life, not that he's discovered exactly what that is as yet, but that it asks the questions why are we here and where are we going. These seem like highly pertinent questions to me and I determine to study philosophy without the perhaps.

At the back of my mind is the white-hot hope that Bill might kiss me. It would not be wrong. It would not be a sin. He isn't my *real* cousin after all. I have had one kissing experience, memorably horrible, after a hop when the boy who had seemed so pleasant suddenly stuffed his tongue into my mouth and halfway down my throat. His saliva revolted me. And Sam Wright did nothing whatsoever, though he always called when he came home from college.

Kissing Bill might be better. We half-scramble down the high field on our way to Tongs Lough. He races the last stretch. We come thundering down to the sandy edge and he reaches the jetty first. A boat with a hole in it lies half-submerged in the shallows, cottony bullrushes pushing through the gash.

"Pity it's smashed," Bill says. "I could've rowed you out a bit."

"Pity. But you'd need to watch out—Wee Menlo might catch us!"

Wee Menlo. The stuff of nightmares. The gnarled waterman who, we believed, haunted the lake throughout our childhood and who nearly snared Rose in his iron grip one autumn afternoon.

"You don't *still* believe in Wee Menlo!" Bill scoffs.

"No. No, of course not, I was joking..." But I believe in the possibility of Wee Menlo as much as I believe in my own life. He is the vile ghoul who lives in dreams, who tickles children to death at night and runs hot on your heels through dark, thorny forests.

"Sit here," I command, tapping the spot beside me on the jetty. I take off my shoes and dip my legs in and out of the water.

81

"This is heaven," says Bill, removing his sandals. His feet are pale and smooth, the toes straight. He lies back and looks at the sky, his feet just catching the water. I look furtively at his face when his eyes are closed. Look. Peer. Closely expose the secrets behind his skin. What I want to do all the time but dare not. In the real world people are forbidden to look too closely. That is one thing I have learned. You get laughed at if you have desires. *Notions* is what Aunt Florence calls them with a superior smile. Kate would not agree. Kate knows that people have feelings.

"Don't mind your Aunt Florrie," she tells Rose and me. "There's more to life than she has ever dreamt of. That's all that's wrong with her."

But the world is full of people like Florrie. The Kates are in short supply, so I learn circumspection, especially at school where girls are harsh and judging.

"That's the way these border people are," Dan says. "They're not given to talking soft."

"Is that why you and Kate got married?"

"Something like that. We're given to talking soft, a pair of softies," he says.

Bill's pupils shrink to pinpricks when he opens his eyes. The irises are flecked green and brown, his lashes long and soft.

"What'll we do?" I enquire.

He stretches like a cat. "I dunno."

"What's it like in college?" I ask, not that interested but eager to get him talking.

"All right. Full of fellows and girls. That kind of thing."

"What kind of thing?"

"What d'you want to know?" he asks, turning towards me with a smile.

I am stuck for a reply. I don't know what I want to know beyond whether he has a girl, and I daren't ask that.

"D'you want to stay *here* then?" I ask.

"Yes. I like to get away. I'm a lazy sod by nature."

I stretch back beside him. We lie for what seems like a long time. I am blissfully happy, absorb the warmth of his shoulder beside mine, catch the warm, clean whiff of his body. It is indefinably male, mixed with a slight odour of perspiration.

"I hope you do study Italian and Philosophy," he says then.

"Yeah?"

"Yep. You'd love it, Hanna."

A silver balloon of joy drifts across my mind. "How many more years have you to go?" I say.

"Two," he says glumly.

"Don't you like it then?"

"Sometimes. My parents think it's great."

Uncle Theo and Aunt Dot christened him Bill because Dot swore that over her dead body would another generation of Bardons have awful, weird names like Theo, Marius and Joachim.

"But what do you think?"

"I dunno. There are other things. Writing maybe. I'm never sure, know what I mean?" He raises himself on one elbow to look into my face. What I know is that he is uncertain but what I know even more strongly is that my body is responding, that my life in these moments has become urgent and excited. The feeling is so delicious and unbearable at once that I look away from his face.

"Hanna?" His left hand moves over mine. Lies gently, as if he is afraid to squeeze it.

"What?" Something strange is happening. His hand

encloses mine completely. I do not withdraw it. For fifteen years I've lived in a naive dream; suddenly I'm catapulted into another world. Our fingers lace. He lies back then, the way we were before. Look at the sky, just as I do. It is marbled and fleecy but the cloud is thin enough for the sun's warmth to penetrate. I nudge in closer. We cannot be seen. The house is obscured by a frieze of trees. *Yes, yes,* I say mentally. *Go on,* I urge him silently.

As if he has heard, he raises himself again and looks at me, leans close as if trying something for the first time, gently places his lips on mine. It is a bird's breath of a kiss, the kind I will never experience again in my life from any man.

"Again?" he says hesitantly. I nod. This time it is longer, and our lips open naturally. Bill's tongue is sweet. It has the hunger and restraint of someone who is unsure. I draw him closer, place my hand to the back of his head and allow my fingers to stroke his hair. I do not want the kiss to stop, but a warning voice tells me I must call a halt to proceedings. Gradually I draw away. His hand is on my breast, light as can be, and my nipples are hard. From Rose's descriptions of boys, I had expected something else, a rampaging animal.

"Let's swim — something — anything!" he says suddenly.

"Yahoo!" I shout in reply, removing my skirt without a thought, forgetting that I am a girl and that people are forever warning girls to be careful. He yahoos back and then we both yahoo across the lake as we undress, our voices echoing back each time. "Yahoo-ooo-ooo!" we yell, making noise to camouflage our excitement, until we are both absolutely naked. We pretend not to look at one another as we jump in, then tread water for a while, out of our depth beyond the jetty.

"Race you out to the middle and back!" I challenge.

He swims fast and well. I do not want to be beaten. I flip over onto my back and start to backstroke, knowing I can easily outstrip him after Kate's summer coaching sessions. The water is quite cold, though the surface is tepid.

"Watch out for Wee Menlo!" he gasps when we're well out from the shore. I shriek, imagine a hand reaching from the depths of the lake to pull me down. Stop swimming, float. The race is over. Bill has won.

"C'mon back, Hanna," he says then, breathlessly.

"Pig," I grumble, moving alongside him in a slower breaststroke.

We are both more tired than we will admit. Close to the jetty he stops and turns, grabs me around the waist. His kiss this time is intense, and my legs go around him as a means of controlling his weight in the water. I am astounded by the hard root at the centre of his body, pull him under, enjoying the game. Then he drags me in turn beneath the surface, all the time moving closer, lower, closer and lower until it happens. I grab the side of the jetty with one hand and balance my weight with my legs around his waist. He forces his way in slowly, with difficulty. We are both gasping, then suddenly he's in me and it hurts but I will not admit to pain, delighted by his pleasure, the pain gradually dissolving and the first ripples of pleasure stirring just as he comes off so suddenly and with such strength that I lose my grip on the jetty and we both sink beneath the water.

For those few moments the world is full of bubbles, dislocated sound, the feel of his limbs and skin as we automatically part before bursting to the surface again.

"Jesus almighty!" he says, springing onto the wooden planks above.

"Fuck me pink!" I say, letting him haul me up beside him.

"I won't answer that," he says, grabbing me again and covering my face in kisses.

"God."

"Are you all right—I mean, I didn't hurt you, did I?"

"No. It was great," I lie, kissing him and hugging him over and over. Beads of water dangle on the tips of his hair, run down his shoulders, his chest, slither in silver rivulets down into the damp nest of hair in his groin.

"We'd better get back soon," I say.

"I'll head back first."

It was going to look funny, the pair of us arriving with our hair wet and clothes damp. He tugs on his underpants, while I pray I'm not pregnant, imagine sperm backstroking like blazes up into me to make me pregnant.

"Do you think we love one another?" I ask, starting to dry myself with my pants.

"I don't know. Perhaps we do."

I wrestle with the implications of this.

"Hanna?"

"What?"

"That was bloody marvellous, wasn't it?" His eyes are shining and again his hands caress me.

"It was."

He smiles and turns, moving up through the slipway towards the trees. He looks back just once. "Yahooo!" he shouts, circling beneath the trees with his arms outstretched. "Yahooo!" I wave, delighted at our password.

The world has changed in an hour. I will go up to the house and we will make small-talk when we want to say much, much more. How am I to explain the wet hair? Uncle Theo and Aunt Dot would take a dim view of such a carry-on if they found out. She in particular, determined to keep Bill in a glass case. If they find out, it will mean the end. The end. Like in a film? Have we had our story? Is that it?

I wait for a longish time, drying out in the sun before

returning, my hair more or less in order again. My watch is ruined, stopped at a quarter past four when I forgot to remove it as we plunged into the water. Finally, I move up through the trees, taking my ease. I wish the day would never end, want time to think about all that has happened, to replay Bill's touches, his soft kisses, his violent hunger. But already the house is in sight, no longer grey the way it used to be but white. The windows of the dining-room are open but, as I look, something about the scene is incongruous. I have a sudden premonition of trouble. Bill has told all, Uncle Theo and Aunt Dot are going bananas, Dan is furious and maybe Kate is dismayed. I feel ashamed and scandalously dirty.

Voices are raised. In the distance, coming closer, the whine of either a fire-engine or an ambulance. I am filled with dread, as always, just as in the night when I expect people to get burnt alive in their homes or illness to strike.

An ambulance turns into our drive, blue lights rotating, slashing the peace of the afternoon. I begin to run, knowing somebody has been taken ill, or even died. Please God don't let it be Dan, oh it cannot be Kate either, please, please God don't let it be them or Rose. I promise to be good, I'll never do it again, I'll never see Bill again, never do the awful thing again, promise, promise, oh God, not them, not any of them.

The hill seems endless as I climb and stumble. The ambulance has reached the door, two men spring quickly out and open the back of the vehicle, taking out a stretcher. I fall into the hallway, out of breath, crying with the knowledge that something dreadful has happened. Real trouble. Dan seems rooted to the spot. Uncle Theo and Aunt Dot, Florrie, Joachim and Lizzie and Bill stand around looking helpless.

"It's all right, Hanna," is the first thing I hear from Bill.

"What's all right? What is it?" I demand angrily.

"It's Rose," says Dan.

"What about her?" My throat dries up. Aunt Florrie comes towards me and puts her arms around my shoulders.

"Rose had an accident, dear, an accident. They're bringing her to the hospital," she says kindly. As always Florrie's manner irritates more than it soothes. "Now, don't you worry your wee head about it, Hanna, she'll be just dandy."

I pull away in a rage, crying. "What's happening, Dan?" I ask.

"The tablets, she took the tablets. My sleepers. Too many — by mistake," he mumbles. I sit down abruptly. There's noise upstairs. Kate's voice. She is repeating something over and over, not shouting, but calmly, as if soothing herself. "It's all right, Rose, you'll be all right, all right, all right..." is what trails down the stairs.

They bring Rose down, strapped into the stretcher. Bill moves to where I am sitting and stands beside me. Nobody says a word as they come down to the hall. She is deathly white with lips purple, as if all the blood had drained from her body. If there was any noise upstairs, it wasn't heard. Kate happened to go up and found her on the bedroom floor, with some of the pills around her. She squeezes my shoulder as they pass. It is like a funeral procession, only worse. I begin to howl aloud. Rose is going to die. Kate goes out the door, telling Dan to follow in the car.

Theo, Dot, Bill and the others remain. Bit by bit I hear. It has something to do with the silver tray, and the order in which our names are inscribed on it. The last thing anybody remembers is that Rose almost knocked it off the dining-room table in a fury, passed some remark about my name coming first when she, Rose, was the eldest and how it wasn't fair. Something like that. Down by the lake Bill and I had forgotten about the tray being presented to Dan and Kate.

I cannot believe that Rose is so jealous. After the meal she had disappeared upstairs sulking, according to Aunt Florrie. She also says that it's time Rose stopped her nonsense and grew up. It is possibly one of the most sensible things ever uttered by Aunt Florrie. The story will not be broadcast to all and sundry but she will be unable to refrain from passing on hints of what happened to certain female friends. In any case it will be all over the town, simply because Rose is being brought into the local hospital where the matron is a renowned backbiter and gossip who would be glad she had one up on Kate.

Poor Rose, is all I can think, terrified she will die. If she does, it won't matter what anybody says; they can bitch and whisper all they want, but if Rose is gone it won't make any difference.

Bill says they'll pump out her stomach. He keeps chatting to me and, although I don't always listen, I know he is trying to make me feel better.

"I once knew a fellow who took an overdose," he says, "and he survived."

"How long before they found him?"

"Oh, hours and hours. Rose's going to be all right, she wasn't asleep for long."

He is the only one who has used the word "overdose." The others are talking about it being an accident.

"Isn't it awful?" says Florrie. "Sure these doctors don't write out the prescription details properly at all. Please God she'll be all right. It was only an accident."

I weep uncontrollably, my nose running, my voice coming in hiccups. Bill offers me his handkerchief. It is warm and damp because his trouser-pocket is still damp from his body. I bury my face in it and close my eyes, enjoying the brief darkness. Despite myself, I smile and, whether Aunt Dot likes it or not, I take his hand in mine and hold on to it. Nobody notices. They are too wrapped up in what has happened.

Chapter Fourteen

—w—

Outside, it is as warm and humid as it was that day. I call the waitress to get the bill. That was the day I became an adult. Two significant things happened. More importantly, the pattern of Rose's life and some of my own responses to things were shaped. More than anybody I know, she has the capacity to milk sympathy and attention from every situation. Even today, with Kate dead, she plays up to Dan. For all I know, her life is more independent now that Kate is gone. For all I know, she is happier. I doubt it though. Kate and Rose loved one another with the fierce possessiveness of two women whose wills conflict on almost everything and whose energies are trained in different ways on the one man. Maybe if Dan had stepped in earlier, it might have made the difference. Maybe if he'd stopped feeling so guilty on account of Rose, for marrying again, for having me. I have always been a mote in Rose's eye.

Over the years Rose's crises have been spectacular. First came the overdose, then the slashed wrists, and after that the crashed car when she was on an LSD trip and thought the vehicle was *Chitty-chitty-bang-bang*, flying all over the world. Her holidays, what she always termed "working trips," frequently ended in crisis and desperate phone calls (collect) home to Dan. She'd been sacked from a restaurant in New

York after saying she agreed with the revisionist historians on Auschwitz and Treblinka. (Things are always made to seem worse than they are, she told the Jewish owner.) Or her latest lover had run off with someone else. Always a misunderstanding, Rose blameless. Much of the panic was designed perhaps unconsciously in the hope of having Kate come running, tearing her hair like a tragic Grecian matriarch. The fact that Kate always reacted calmly has frustrated Rose. Finally, her abortion, a *fait accompli* before Christmas one year. Even up to the time of Kate's death, few conversations took place in the old house in which Rose's problems did not pop up. Rose this and Rose that. Poor Rose, has she enough money? Poor Rose, I hope that new boyfriend is good to her. Our parents, as Dan once said to me, were a pair of softies.

Rose has kept them running. She resisted Kate from the start, my mother and not hers, relentlessly testing her, even into adulthood. That I cannot forgive because it has been so wasteful. I loathe attention-seekers, cannot join in the glib sympathy, the platitudes which slip easily from people's mouths when they talk about people who mismanage their lives.

I pay my bill and leave a tip for the waitress. "Make sure *she* gets it," I instruct the cashier, pointing to the acerbic wench who served me, taking a green mint from the little saucer. Out on the street there are swirls of dust, traffic-fumes, heat.

Life bears down no matter which way you turn. Like something giving birth to itself, over and over. Amazing how things come back year after year, the way almost nothing is so final that it can wipe out the habit of living. Nature never tires, nothing short of a Hiroshima will snuff it out. That's the sort of rhetoric those of a religious bent love to go on about. They can draw on that and they feel better. Today I am so tired that the thought of nature replenishing itself exhausts me.

Another statistic. Suicides peak twice yearly. There's the Christmas batch when people are either toute seule for the festivities or else when whole families inflict the discontents of the past year on one another until one of their number decides not to play ball any more. Ergo, cut wrists, overdoses, drownings. The other peak is in early summer. The growing and blooming, the frilly cherry and almond trees, whitethorn like mad runnels of cotton criss-crossing the countryside, elderflower, cow parsley and Queen Anne's Lace. Makes a certain type crumble. That I can understand. Yet that's the difference between my sister and me. She cultivates the extreme, whereas I'm competent and get on with life (with one or two lapses into self-violation in recent times). She reaps sympathy for outrageous behaviour while I earn a certain amount of envy, and occasionally outright jealousy, from those who assume that living comes easier to me.

Yet for the first time in our lives, for the past few months Rose and I have seen each other in a new light, have shed much of the old friction through the discovery of something shared — our panda-bear destinies. I imagine us both in our seventies, two cantankerous old bats, holding out to the last. There's no question about it, Rose won't bow out like a character in a melodrama. Not she. She will have an entourage to the end, people to worry about her.

Grafton Street streams with mid-afternoon shoppers and drifters, cars and buses having been long banished to surrounding road-systems. Bookshops where Dan and I browsed twenty years back are stuffed with luminous clothing. Benetton, Oui-set, Ton-Sur-Ton, colour co-ordinated Escada, Laurel, Blackie. Part of the pleasure of any trip from Clonfoy to Dublin for the day was the inevitability of ending up in some bookshop or other with Dan, when half an hour would pass easily as we turned pages in silence. Today, what was once the Eblana bookshop is a hairdresser's, full of flouncing, busy-looking young men and women.

Crowds obstruct. Street-musicians attract them like bees near flowers. At least three different types of music compete for attention. The nearest source is a blues trio using the acoustics of an overhanging shop facade to make their sound more impressive. Billie Holliday, throttled again. People stand about, looking bashful. Some throw silver into the box and pass on.

Just above Bewley's a guitarist makes a mess of Scott Mackenzie's "San Francisco." The man's fingers have not mastered the intricacies of the piece but he battles on regardless. Meanwhile his girlfriend moves smilingly around with a cap in hand, a gormless young woman who no doubt believes she's supporting a great artist. Why hasn't she got her own guitar? And why isn't lover boy collecting for her?

The Diceman stands stock-still, his face painted in gold lustre, his entire head shorn and also golden, the eyes emphasised by purple kohl, lips exaggerated by cupid points in bright red. Arms folded across his chest, he wears the attire of an exotic sultan, minus turban. People press close and try to distract him but he never flinches. Occasionally he winks and they draw back, briefly unsettled by the fact that he is alive, that he observes, that he can choose such control.

Mountebanks, troubadours, dancers, beggars, mutants. A woman with a twisted face in Johnson Court, aware of shoppers with money to spend, shoppers with change. They create the ambience so beloved by tourists the world over, lend what people imagine is spontaneity to proceedings. Everything has its price, can be strait-jacketed and sold as the original of the species. Authenticity to whet the appetites of the sated.

I am familiar with ambivalence. At work, press releases pour in prior to shoots. In my pigeonhole every week a neat bundle of hyperbole. Inside, in the newsroom, the sound of life with an urgent capital L bursts importantly through the doorway. Current affairs, politics, foreign news. That's where it's at, sexy stories, to use the current phrase. The heavy photographers do the political scoops, arrivals and departures of foreign dignitaries. I persuade the editor of the necessity of my covering Paris twice a year but he refuses to give way on the Milan spring collections. The nation's media snored gently at home on Christmas Day 1989 while Romania seethed and new air filled Europe's ancient lungs. That's the funny thing about press people. We often miss the real human drama, convinced we know best.

I have failed, I have failed, I have failed most grievously to be content. The skeleton of the world has been stripped of its flesh and every preview I shoot, every actor I arrange, every model, every press release tells me that there is some terror at the heart of existence. Why this should be is a mystery. Why should I not expect to be happy? Why is happiness not a natural state, a right even? It is enshrined as a perfectly valid pursuit in the American constitution, which is one reason I like Americans. Such hope! Such innocence! They will land on Mars before the century is out. What adds to the confusion is the determined gaiety, the adamantine mask of humour donned by so many acquaintances. There is a famous Munch painting called *The Scream*. I love it.

The notion of performance is not objectionable as such. We must all protect ourselves. Certain things would not be understood by strangers, so some guise is called for. That's why turtles have shells and hedgehogs have sharp spines. But some people are hell-bent on displays of autonomy, on being the life and soul of whatever party they belong to.

When I began working, I was really keen every time I had to go out. Expectant was what you'd call it. And Sam used to come with me. But how enthusiastic I was, how forward-looking, as if every fashion-show, every photocall, held the promise of complete understanding. A key to existence in the composition of a photograph. The darkroom was a sanctuary then. Today it still holds a subversive peace. The bloody infra-reds, the acrid odours, that occult moment when light does its work and an image is lifted from the tray's compounds. I behold myself, supreme alchemist, goddess of positive and negative contours, form the whole world with my eyes and fingers!

Funny thing though: now I have difficulty telling the difference between what goes on on the ramp at a fashion-show, or in a theatre, and what happens elsewhere. Life and art inseparable and indistinguishable. Bullshit. Life is the thing. Life is the *leac-liath*, the grey, viscous dirt through which I am created and made flesh. The fact that I can barely tell the difference between the two shows a hiatus.

Each press-release assures the photographer of a spectacle *par excellence*. There is no superlative to describe adequately the brilliance of the actors, the avant-garde quality of B's latest fashion collection which was inspired by his experiences with the tribes of the Amazon basin or the importance of the opening of refurbished inner-city buildings. Inevitably the not-to-be-missed event is soporific, the building hideous, B's capsule collection an embarrassment and the leading actor rushes his lines during the photocall, which causes the director to lose his temper.

There's nothing more satisfying than doing transparencies for plays produced on a shoestring. The press release is a botched Gestetner job, there are minimal advance plaudits and I've never heard of the actors. The less

95

known they are, the more careful they tend to be, the more inspired the production (provided, of course, that they are not deluded). The solitary endeavour works wonders for passion.

The windows of a marble-fronted shop are filled with mannequins. Two pictures are presented to the eye: the outdoor one and the evening or cocktail one. Each is structured to look like a scene from real life. The mannequins suggest how people should look and behave. The outdoor figures have long, long legs, slender arms and curving, impossibly long fingers like Thai dancers. Length is everything. They are outfitted in sporty summer numbers: natty little jackets with naval braiding at the shoulders and cuffs. The look is a red, white and navy one. Tried and trusted. New designs, same classical colours. I wonder if Sandrine would approve. The cocktail scene catches my attention. One token man stands among four women, complete with slightly bulging crotch and stubble on his designer face. His purpose is to provide a centrepiece around which they can twirl and pirouette in flouncy peplumed silk, strapless black, backless, frontless seduction outfits.

Aha! Hanna Troy. Growing bitter. That must not happen. I catch sight of my reflection in a window. I glare at the mannequins, then walk slowly along the glass arcade of the shop's alluring entrance.

Chapter Fifteen

—⚊⚊—

Christmas 1982, and Sam wants to buy me a dress. We've just left a bookstore where I bought him five books on glass, its genesis and possibilities. The department-store assistant is pushy. Hot and flustered, I'd have preferred a complete surprise to a dress, but as usual we were short of time and, for the sake of observing ritual, decided to buy each other gifts. I select a simple lacy dress with a kick-pleat at the back, shunning the gaudy confections on display around me. Christmas music drifts on the air: "White Christmas," "Santa Claus Is Coming to Town."

Sam regards the dress with a look of dismay on his face. "What about this one?" he asks, pointing to a green and black polka-dot garment which to my mind would look better on a Christmas-tree fairy.

"No. Wouldn't suit me," I say decisively.

"Ah, Hanna, it's Christmas for Christsake!"

He sees you when you're sleeping. "But I prefer the other one," I tell him.

"Get it then—if that's what you want," he says in resignation.

"Don't you like it at all?"

"Since you ask—no. It's too..." He searches for the word, "too old for you."

He rummages through the racks. A rare moment. Sam in the women's section of a department store. *He knows when you're awake.* Sam, who prefers glass models, the sight of a well-planned development, a new housing complex or business-centre, who spends his time looking at architraves and cornices, gauging levels, selecting cladding.

"This." He is quite definite. It is black, slinky, with a double row of diamante running from cleavage-level down. I examine the price-tag. It is exorbitant. *You better watch out, you better not shout.*

"Where would I wear it?" I do not want to admit that his choice is so obviously better than mine. *So be good for goodness sake.* I am dazed by the crowds, the clash of reds and greens, snakes of tinsels, the aroma of sandalwood.

Chapter Sixteen

—ɯ—

I regret not having bought that dress. Little things like that were the beginning of the end. Point-scoring. The inability to give in once in a while. The utter determination to be right at all costs. None better than I at pressing my own sense of rightness to the bitter end. Damn him. There's no point parroting his point of view. I'm sick of Sam's moderation, his concessions to liberalism. The voices of men I know and have known echo in my head. Even Bill's. Everything prefixed with a warning. *You must be careful not to go too far. The danger is that extremism will push things too far.* Well, bully for extremism.

There is little on this street not designed to con, fool and generally make an eejit of the average woman, from hairdressers to clothing establishments and accessories shops. I continue walking and consider how throughout the world there are women whose husbands are perfectly content, husbands who do not necessarily love their wives but who have forged an understanding. The thing is workable. I believe to this day that Sam loved me. He may still do. It has not been so long, after all. In time who knows what could happen? The situation is complicated by Sandrine and — no, I will not think of that just now. If I can get over this malaise, if I can seal up the fissures, I shall be able to get on with life again, fervently, ardently.

Yet I grow angry to think of those other women. In suburbs or in the country. Those who have forged an understanding.

In the Australian bush or Nigeria or in the hill country of northern Thailand, beyond Chiang-Mai. The majority work something out.

The message from the shop windows is clear. Buy me. I will make you desirable. I will lead you to the man of your dreams, will facilitate the earth-shattering orgasm with the most silk-skinned lover. His rod will conduct you magically beyond the drab confines of this city to a place of excitement and unending delight. Another message goes with this one. The exhortation to good behaviour. Good women, nice women, *real* women, dress like this, and this, and this...All around the windows glint, mannequins smile smugly. For a moment my hands stiffen. I'd like to lob an axe through those polished glass panes.

Sam always worried about things going *too far* when I got excited about something, an idea perhaps, a book I'd read, people's behaviour. "These things can get carried too far," he used to say. You can never go far enough. Never, never, never. Something which many women know, though they do little enough about it; which men know too but because they need to control things a bit, make limited use of.

My stomach rumbles at the smell of coffee as I pass Bewley's a second time. Inside, sounds of intimate conversation hint at relaxation and retreat. My hatred for Sam wells up again. He should have seen about it. He should have gone to a doctor. For me. That is what hurts. He wouldn't do it. As if he were trying to get the better of me by not acknowledging the problem. The moron. Letting me carry on, wondering, suspecting. If only he'd admitted it, we could have availed of some other course of action. But he never wanted it that way either. All along, he rejected something in

100

me. That was the only way he could show it. In some way I made him feel impotent. Now he has all the power he could wish. How he has shown me! How he has proven just how well he can manage! We will never be like Mark and Anna, our lives filled with mundane annoyances: school-bus times, homework, play, disturbed nights and early mornings, delighted screams on Christmas morning. The knowledge of the silence that accompanies us at the root of our lives is ever present, just as it is present for everybody but people like us hear it earlier. Whispering. Mocking. Reminding us of final limitations, denying us the simplest of fleshly vanities, the prospect of seeing ourselves mirrored in the set of a mouth perhaps.

At the bottom of Grafton Street I use the Pass machine. I press the button opposite £80 and wait while the machine goes through its clunking motions. Money finally slides through a chink, followed by the card and lastly a receipt. To my surprise I'm flush in credit. Sam is using other sources, leaving me to the old account. A further sign of his independence. Despite bravado about not needing him, my throat contracts and I would like to put my head down and sob. Instead I make my way towards an art gallery, walking briskly to conceal my despair.

Chapter Seventeen

—ᘏᘏ—

In the final months, Kate paints. Visiting us at weekends, she arrives equipped, ready to draw on every resource. She and Sam get along fine nowadays. He is naturally tolerant of visual artists.

Kate's self-portrait from years back hangs in our bedroom now. She gave it to Sam after he admired it. It has adorned the wall over the bed for ten years. I would not part with it for anything; I have finally learnt to read that awkward clownish expression, the clouded eyes, the mouth a meniscus smile that could be a grimace.

Our present conspiracy to keep our families from knowing the truth is a feat of mendacity. Everything is fine, we assure them, fine and dandy. Sam and I compete as never before. Both of us are determined to win, to be right at any cost, but small things betray us.

We do the household shopping turn and turn about. If I forget something on the list, he reminds me; if he forgets the pear and apricot spread or the biodegradable washing-powder, I strike back.

This time he has bought in food for the bank holiday weekend. We hate such occasions. Kate and Dan are coming but that is not the reason for our hate; it is rather that we dread the protracted hours in which people jolly one another along and the added penance of a Monday when the shops are shut. As usual we have not arranged to travel. This is a mutual decision based on the fact that we do not want to hear diverse Dublin accents over in the West.

Before Kate and Dan's arrival, I have been feeling particularly morose; I would like to walk out, be far removed from Sam's tensions. The car pulls into the driveway. Kate is driving.

"I might not be for this earth much longer but I'm not going to cut things any shorter than necessary!" she says. Dan gets excited behind the wheel. He is no longer safe to drive with, being easily distracted by fields of cattle, new houses, speeding drivers and complicated turn-offs from motorways. His attempts at parking make Kate impatient, which confuses him further. He drifts past space after space, circles buildings at least twice before selecting an appropriate spot. By then Kate is red-faced and sarcastic.

"Mind now, you might do something dangerous!" she'll say.

Today she has taken command and turns smartly into our drive, brakes quickly and pulls up the handbrake. There's a lot of rummaging through the back seat; doors open and slam shut. They bring enough gear for a month. Kate carries the case. She is still strong, despite the yellow tint of her complexion. Dan comes towards us jerkily, loaded down with bits and pieces. A heavy overcoat and a light one on one arm, German *Wanderschuhe* and lighter walking ones held in the other. A Brown Thomas bag dangles from the little finger of his left hand, holding pipes and tobaccos, spectacle-case, and suntan-oil in case the sun shines.

In recent years he has become a sun-worshipper and a hill-walker, and he also experiments with new tobaccos wherever he travels. He has reached a stage in life where he expects some reward for his endeavours as a parent, some sign of interest gained despite depreciation. He frequently raves about King Lear and his daughters in mock-dramatic tones and asks if there is any man more unfortunate than he. This is usually with regard to Rose, but occasionally I am the cause, as when he feels one of my prints has broken the limits of privacy. Funeral photos. My sole expedition to England, the burial of Corporal X who was booby-trapped in the North.

Kate is depressed. I can tell by the fact that she has brought her paints and easel. I am so devastated at the thought of her death that I have scarcely allowed myself to consider it, even though we talk openly about what is happening. Which is what she wants. She has asked to be buried in the orchard at home and has already disposed of some of her possessions, dividing her rings between Rose and me. Turquoise and pearl for her, amethyst for me.

But in films and stories it happens like this: the woman whose mother is dying would have some consolation in the discovery that she is newly pregnant. The circle of living made complete. A life for a death. Hope. A new beginning from the blind-ends of Kate's life. That's how it would be. Only that morning, a Friday, I am about to tell Sam that we might have good news. I am five days overdue. That can mean only one thing. My mind races, try as I might to contain the excitement. I play and replay scenes I would like to experience, some realistic, others fanciful. I imagine telling Sam. His reaction. There's an ad on television which fascinates me. The husband comes in to breakfast and there in his cereal bowl is a tiny pair of white bootees. He is overjoyed and incredulous, rushes his wife to the nearest seat and holds her as if she were a treasure. Most women like to feel as if they are precious, held high.

Another ad, for a brand of tea, shows the man pacing anxiously outside the delivery ward, a good old-fashioned approach: no gawking, husband kept at a safe distance. Next thing the nurse comes out with one on each arm. Twins! Abundant fertility. Meanwhile the wife lies back sipping a refreshing cup of tea. Then the razor-blade ad. Having kids is the done thing, in that all the marketing media love the idea of it. Having kids *sells* things. This hunk in the razor-blade ad is an all-rounder. Races cars, jogs, works and fathers. Lovely one-second subliminal shot of him holding naked infant.

This time, in real life, I felt as if something had happened. Slightly different. Taut. Full-breasted. A pleasant heaviness. But by lunchtime it had begun. I bled and bled. No doubt now. Hanna Troy getting older by the month, drying up year after year, wasted, unfinished.

I try to talk to Sam, who is studying plans from the office.

"What?" he says irritably.

"I feel terrible." What I want to say is "Tell me you love me. I need you. I am frightened." Instead I utter the last bit quietly.

"What're you frightened of now?" he asks almost wearily.

"I thought I was pregnant. This morning. But I'm not." My voice is clipped. I begin to weep. He comes over but I turn from him furiously, disappointed that we cannot do *something*, enraged that he is obstructing things.

"I'm all right, leave me..." I whisper. He withdraws. Another nail in the coffin.

Outside it is summer. Early summer. We are on the cusp of April and May. Hawthorn and chestnut breathe perfumes on the air; the birds are going crazy. The blackbird on the top of our birch screeches with joy, revelling in life's loveliness. If only it could have been true, this once. It would bring all kinds of forgiveness. Remove our angers, dry the scalding tears. My sorrow whips itself up to such a heat that I would like to float away. Down the Nile. In the dark. In one of those long papyrus boats, hidden between the rushes, looking at the moon. I would like release. The door closes and he is gone. I listen as his footsteps sound blankly on the stairs.

Later, voices carry in a muffled way up through the floorboards. Our house has shortcomings and advantages. The rooms are large and difficult to heat. On Sam's insistence, the old dry-rotted staircase was ripped out and replaced with a spiral that runs up through the house into the attic. This he transformed, making a magnificent dark-room on one side and on the other a sunroom which has an airy view over all the roofs, and the gardens as they tumble towards the river. On the other hand, it is a long house, the main bedrooms are well separated, and there is none of the rabbit-hutch feel common to many homes. Already Kate has established her base in the second spare bedroom and she paints heedless of what is going on, having set up her canvas below the broad windows. I need to talk to her. The door is ajar. I push and watch.

She has not heard. Instead, she sits layering her canvas with a thick gunge of yellow, the palette-knife cutting and dabbing with confidence. It's remarkable, because she had no training as a young person—the entire family's energies were ever bent on day-to-day practicalities: running a large household, buying cattle. What she produces now is quite respectable, if occasionally too illustrative; so they tell me, people I meet. Kate has exhibited; one critic from a national newspaper wrote a bilious diatribe but the others were moderately welcoming. Kate did not give a damn, either way.

"What're you working on?"

She doesn't turn around. "Poppies."

"Why all the yellow?"

"I'll be adding purple," she replies vaguely.

"What about red?"

"In time. Have to build things up first," she says.

"Kate?" She doesn't answer, my patience snaps. "Mother'." I call, as if to remind her of who she is. She turns suddenly, as if she had indeed almost forgotten, as if the word conjured some inconsequential apprenticeship in the past which has nothing to do with her current state.

"How old were you when you had me?" I know the answer of course.

"Thirty. A good age."

"I'm well past that." I tug at the pillowcase frills, sit on the small bed.

"No matter. Many a flower was born to blush unseen and waste its sweetness or whatever," she replies, raising her head appraisingly towards the canvas.

"What does that mean?" I demand, getting to my feet. She hasn't even noticed my face, which is blotched and puffy.

"I think it means that some people have talents which go unappreciated."

"Wrong context, I think," I answer grimly.

She stops to consider, then nods. "You're right. Wrong quotation in the wrong place."

I try again. "Nothing's happening." She turns to regard me. Her face is thoughtful; yet she has not grasped my meaning.

"Plenty of time for that yet," she answers briskly. "You worry too much."

"There isn't plenty of time and why shouldn't I worry?" I am sick to the teeth of being told not to worry, to relax, to forget myself. What else is a human mind and body for if not to remember, to be aware and to live in conflict?

"You've got Sam. He's a good man."

"Sam won't have the test done, for God's sake!"

She sounds remote and curious at once. "Has he said that?"

107

"Yes."

"And there's nothing wrong in your department?"

"Nothing they can discover."

"Sometimes it takes a while to uncover these things. They might find something yet." Then, as an afterthought, "And you know what men are like, dear. Proud. So proud."

I leave the room and go downstairs. How they protect Sam! He and Dan are chatting over the top of their newspapers.

"Florrie isn't well," Dan informs me.

"What's wrong with her?" I snap. They're a pack of dying flies as far as I'm concerned. Let them damn well get on with it.

"Tumour," he says, taking a swig of whiskey.

"Can it be removed?"

He nods. "There'll be complications afterwards. She might be different, but they don't know for sure at the hospital."

The whole world is dying. At school, that's what the nuns would have said. It was incomprehensible then. How could you live and die at the same time? One of those neat little existential tricks for which we all have a talent? Hard to imagine Aunt Florrie laid out in a hospital bed, never mind a coffin. Years ago, I thought she and all the rest would go on for ever and ever, adorning my life and Rose's like props in a drama in which we led very significant lives.

When people are rowing, very ordinary communication assumes aggravating dimensions of tone and nuance.

"Sam, where's the Parmesan?" I know he's forgotten to buy it.

"Behind you. On the shelf," he says with calculated coolness.

"It's all gone," I insist.

"Then I'll go and get some," he replies.

"Leave it. I'll make do with Cheddar."

Dan is immersed in his newspaper at the far end of the room.

"Don't martyr yourself!" Sam hisses quietly.

"That's your style, darling," I remark, banging the saucepan.

Bollocksfuckimanyway.

By the time everything is ready, the house is filled with the fragrance of cheese and garlic. Sam has washed one of his organic lettuces, has chopped organic chives and tossed together a dressing of cider vinegar and virgin olive oil. Nothing but the best for him. A life streamlined to accommodate any new departures in the environmental movement. We have three different litter bins: one for tins, one for plastics and one for left-over food. Humus is what Sam calls it, after he piles the biodegradables in a corner of the garden, along with grass-cuttings and bits of pruned shrubs left for sorting by the gardener who comes in about three times a year to do the heavy stuff.

The house is full of environmental literature from the diehard types with whom he corresponds. I am sympathetic to most of them. What I find obnoxious is his long-running correspondence with three grain-eating, mandala-gazing cranks from the far side of the country. Every week we receive a thick wad of closely printed waffle. They are probably among the first to take the Greenhouse Effect and the Nuclear Winter seriously. These cranks have the right idea, and now they have been proven correct in their warnings, even if they pay too much attention to a paranoid German physicist who claimed he could make grass grow in the Arizona desert. He also claimed that sterility was caused by frozen energies locked in the pelvic muscles.

Week after week Sam reads this pulp. Recently they sent

some extra information. The woman of the trio had just given birth to a first child, the issue of a genital embrace (their term) of such stupendous quality that conception could be the only result. We have already read about her feelings during this well-mapped pregnancy, how she avoided the necessity for an episiotomy by the simple act of massaging her perineum with olive oil twice daily. I double up at the hilarity of it. But Sam is every bit as bad as they are. How I want to abuse him. How I'd like to beat him black and blue this evening, the pig-headed fool.

"Get the wine, would you?" I say. "It's still in the car."

He is clearly at the end of his tether. His face stiff and unyielding, eyes icy, beyond appeal. He would like to let fly but I will not let him — know he will not attempt it in the presence of Sam and Kate. Kate wanders downstairs just as he goes outside to fetch the wine. She still pretends to feel hunger but merely rearranges the food on her plate. Sam has not reappeared by the time the meal is served.

Dan helps himself to salad. "Good greens, these," he says appreciatively. He has poured himself a second whiskey. "Have some, dear," he tells Kate. She eyes them doubtfully. Her stomach has shrunk, half of it already removed.

"Go on — a little — you need to keep your strength up," he cajoles. His eyes are blue and kindly. To look at them fills me with remorse.

"Where the hell's Sam got to?" I tut.

"Ah, give the fellow a chance — he's trying to find the bottle," says Dan, putting too much food on Kate's plate. She does not refuse it but sits staring at it as if she is bracing herself.

"Sam!" I call from the doorway.

"Coming!" he shouts from the car. He closes the door slowly and makes to come up the path, the bottle of red swinging from his left hand. Just as I warn him to be careful, the bottom of the bottle catches the low granite wall that runs along one side of the house. If he had cut the glass mechanically it could not have been neater. The whole bottom falls free and with it the wine explodes in a wide splatter over his trousers and feet, sinking redly into the paving. In frustration he smashes the rest of the bottle against the wall. Transfixed, I watch the wine on his feet, how it settles in seconds in hairline crevices between his toes, at the base of his toenails and in a lurid pink gash across the tan leather of his sandals. He doubles over on his hunkers as if to pick up the pieces. I do not pity him but am afraid that he will not accept sympathy from me right now.

"It's all right," I tell him, kneeling. "Really. It's all right, Sam," I repeat, knowing that for a moment anyway I have him within my span. I reach out and clasp both his hands in mine, tightly. His face shivers, his mouth trembles, the lower lip held tightly, a vein in his forehead pulsing. He stands up. I kiss him on the cheek, then bend, picking splinters of glass from the front of his trousers.

More than anything I regret my earlier feelings of violence, the foul language in my head. He kisses me back, on the mouth. It is the first time we have kissed like this in a week. He goes upstairs. When I return to the kitchen, Kate and Dan do not seem to have noticed anything amiss. She has picked her way through dinner, Dan helps himself to another serving of everything.

A truce is reached. That night we make love. Dan and Kate are at the other end of the house. (After we married, Sam and I found it difficult to make love in our former homes, under the parental roof where too many ghosts were liable to hover at the bottom of our bed, regarding, reproving, frowning.) They move in and out, shut doors with a vigorous slam, my father doing push-ups on the bathroom floor, Kate coughing. As her health wanes, his thrives rudely.

There are few preliminaries.

"I have my period."

"I don't care, just let me in," he murmurs, "let me in to that soft, wet cave." As we move and stretch there comes a release from limitations, as if we have said something important, though not a word of what could be called conversation passes our lips. Our love-language is punctuated by little gasps, by private words which make no sense. There is indescribable happiness to be had with the right man in your arms at the right moment. That is how I feel as our movements become more urgent and the waves of pleasure mount.

When finished, we are plastered in blood. His chest, my breasts, our stomachs. It is dark and heavy. His fingers carry it as he strokes my face. I reach down and cover my fingers with it, then trace a mark with two fingers across his forehead, down the bridge of his nose and across his cheekbones, bless him with the tang of menstruation. Sam has relaxed. His anger has evaporated. For the first time comes the realisation that it might be possible to let go of the desire to have a child. What I still cannot acknowledge, though, is Sam's blindness, his unwillingness to recognise that I am fertile. In his arms I feel safe. I am with my own man, who has just made love to me, who has needed to be inside me above all others because I offer something none other can.

We have met people in similar situations on holiday. We are not as unique as we feel in this country. In Turkey I had a conversation with a street-vendor who was more than sympathetic. Sam waited at a teahouse further along while I bought some shorts. The vendor had no children and his wife had left him and returned in disgrace to her family in Ankara. That evening a man offered to shine Sam's shoes.

"I have wife and seven cheeldrin!" he moaned.

Progeny or its absence is always a useful conversational topic in certain parts of the world. In Tunisia the dark-lashed Berber women value fertility above everything. In Asia some Buddhists performed a bag ceremony for us, wreathing our wrists with white cotton string, showering us with good wishes for health, fertility and well-being.

Lying in bed now, I think that Sam and I need a ceremony. The night is dark and still. Outside the headlights of passing cars arc along the wall and disappear. Neon light flickers from a restaurant further down the road. We could be in a 1940s Bogart movie, two lovers in a sparsely furnished room barely lit by yellow and pink neon from some joint.

We need ritual. We need acknowledgement. There are things that should be said. Otherwise our lives will never be celebrated. Sam will never be a paterfamilias and nothing I know — no skill, no moment of light captured — will be passed on. Growing old will be quite meaningless without young people somewhere on the peripheries of our lives. So there should be some ceremony, some alternative little knees-up which would praise the good things in our lives.

The next morning Dan is up and about, splashing in the bathroom. My tongue feels thick and my lips are sealed, as always happens after the deep sleep that accompanies an energetic sexual interlude.

"Oh my God," Sam groans, sitting up, but grinning.

I drift back to sleep, and when I awake he's beside me, with a trayful of breakfast. Tea in a huge blue cup and lots of buttered toast. He smells fresh and washed.

Kate paints for most of the weekend. Her stomach has ceased troubling her. Dan thinks that's a sign that the end is near. So do I. On Monday he weeps surreptitiously into the pages of a novel. I have stockpiled my grief, have no idea what hair-trigger moment will cause it to tumble forth.

Later we take a drive. A new bridge outside the city, part of a modern ring-road system, is to be opened the following day. Members of the public are allowed to walk across this sacred object in order to take photographs because it has cut right across the river valley in one of the county's most scenic routes. The place is Anameala or Ath na Meala, the Honey Ford, where bees were once supposed to have dammed the Liffey with golden wax to stop Viking marauders from plundering a nearby monastery. I've done some work on this urban disaster, photographed a recently destroyed pre-Christian burial ground which was unearthed during the sinking of the support pylons. The photograph drew the usual responses in the letters columns: for and against, the righteous and shocked versus the pragmatic.

Hundreds of people cluster on the bridge. Sam has been in almost jovial good form all day, in so far as he has ever been jovial, humouring Kate by standing for an hour as she sketches him in her room.

Dan links her and they cross the bridge behind us. Once out in the centre, the wind gusts up the valley and they turn back because of the cold. Sam takes a few shots of the view, then suddenly turns the camera on me. I smile easily and directly at the camera because I am in love with him again. I want to speak to him, to tell him everything, to have everything come all right.

It is Kate's first and last visit to the bridge at Anameala, and all through it Dan rambles on about Rose. She has recently introduced them to Erkus, the Corkman who owns a petshop in Ranelagh. Dan cannot understand how anybody from Cork can be called Erkus.

114

"What kind of a name is that for a fellow?" he demands, peering over the bridge and out into the valley. "He can't be from Cork," he insists.

"He is," says Sam.

"What'd you expect? Miah? Finbarr?" I ask.

"That's not the point," says Dan.

He objects to the fact that Rose has chosen to live with Erkus instead of getting married. "He's a chancer!" he rants, struggling to light a pipe in the wind as we make our way back to the car. "Him and his petshop! And his bald spot!"

"Appearances don't matter," Kate cuts in with a trace of her old assertiveness. A sheen of perspiration has broken out on her forehead.

"To hell with that! He hasn't got a proper job, they're living as man and wife and she hasn't got a job either, apart from two-bit parts in this theatre business!"

Dan favours security. He forgets that Rose is in her early forties, forgets that she is a grown, a middle-aged woman. There have, after all, been mistakes. We have picked her up and dusted her down, paid her debts, used contacts to get her work. I bailed her out of a police-station in the middle of the night when she was hauled in for drunken driving. Another time Sam found the injured cat she had thrown downstairs in a drunken fury. Its ribs were fractured.

But Dan lives in terror of Kate's dying, of Rose's unpredictability. I would like to think he has a terror for me too but can never be sure or even of how greatly I matter. In his eyes I am competent, married, parcelled up and out of the way. They drive off that evening, having packed away clothes, fragments, Dan's pipes, books, tobacco, coats and shoes, none of which was used. Kate is truly tired. When they have left, the house falls silent. Sam's contentment has not evaporated, however; what happened between us was real and healing.

He is in the garden, weeding the vegetable drills.

"Coffee?" I call through the window.

He nods. "The decaffeinated," he shouts over his shoulder.

Typical. The evening sun catches the top of his head as he bends over baby beetroots and tiny threads of chives and scallions. It turns his hair to a rich, burnished brown. The garlic is up. This year he planted it in a circle. Some old wives' tale about its growing better when planted in the round rather than in rows. I turn to make coffee but the phone rings. It is Sandrine. We exchange pleasantries and she asks for Sam. I call him again and get the cups out. Kate has left behind her sketch of Sam. It is jerky, as is her style, but accurate in its unevenness. A thick-haired big man with a puzzled face. I decide to frame it, half-listening as he answers Sandrine monosyllabically, wondering vaguely what she wants.

Chapter Eighteen

—◊—

Kate's funeral is one of the worst things that has ever happened. Dan is incoherent. Rose sobs. Some people have an inbuilt knack of coping with situations through daunting displays of emotion. Others simply faint. Sam and I stand wordless but I wish I could faint.

She insisted on being buried in the orchard. It has caused hair tearing among the Bardons. Who ever heard of such a thing in Clonfoy? Burial in unconsecrated ground, no less. But a dying woman's wishes are to be respected, no matter that the local clergy are somewhat miffed. An old priest friend of Dan's from a western island agrees to perform the interment.

The orchard is where the dead cats and dogs and injured birds of some thirty years are buried. A splendid plum tree waves luxuriantly in the lower corner. Each year it throws out scented Victorias, pink-fleshed with hints of yellow. The place is neglected and the trees old. Smells are of decay and mulchy earth. The trees have not been pruned since before Dan and his first wife took over the property; the branches are thick and mossy, so strong an adult could easily straddle them.

Kate composed a poem for the occasion. My cousin Bill, who became a poet, reads for us. Joachim and Theo and Florrie are present. There are wives and husbands, cousins and aunts from Clonfoy and beyond, plus Kate's arty friends.

People clear their throats and shuffle as Bill reads what Kate has written, "...and if grasses whimper, that is not my sorrow, if leaves fall it signals no death..." None of which provides the least consolation for Rose and me. Erkus stands at her side, strokes her hair every so often. He is expressive, just like Rose. His brows are drawn intently together and his hair is tonsured like that of a medieval monk. His movements are precise and elegant. In the distance, their two Alsatians are baying. They accompany them everywhere, even though they were bought as watchdogs after the petshop was broken into some months beforehand. They would have been brought to the orchard were it not for Florrie remarking that there was a place for everything.

It is a freezing cold January day. Kate lasted right through the summer and autumn. She took to her bed in December, told Dan that she was tired and never rose again. There was no need for hospital. Rose and I managed, though we could hardly watch the sight of so much deterioration. Kate's skin had the sallow, waxen look of the cancer patient; cheeks which were once full and smooth had retracted, hugged deep into the hollows below her cheekbones. I was calm, which is not to say that we avoided discussing the imminent event. She would have hated that, was never one for burying truths, ignoring realities.

"But I feel guilty!" I remember saying one day as she sat on the edge of the bed, wrapped in a purple kimono which Rose had brought home. Kate shifted uncomfortably, her head hanging forward weakly.

"You must never feel guilty until you have actually committed a crime," she wheezed. "You're staying, I'm going, that's all there is to it and—" She paused to take another slow breath. "—as long as we all love one another..." Her voice faded away, and I left the room for a few minutes, in an effort to prevent my eyes from overflowing with tears.

At least it is winter. I could not bear to think of keeping her anniversary in coming years in high summer. This is most appropriate. A north wind like knives, clouds adding the sense of steel, brushing the hills around Clonfoy, and there is nothing would convince me that this world is for the living.

All through the burial in the orchard I remember the things she said.

"Never, ever, crush the vulnerable!" she would rant, lighting a fresh Sobranie for herself and offering Rose one. We were that sort of family. No sort really. We just *were*, together for a time, rooted and secure with Kate, who kept us perplexed in a pleasant and interesting way because she knew something about the goodness of living.

Theo and Joachim have aged in recent years. Joachim's wife, Lizzie, died ten years ago and he lives with his eldest son, a farming bachelor. Between them they make out, having organised a system of survival in the way that solitary men do. Theo still takes photographs but his daughter makes magnificent holographs and exhibits her work all over the place. Aunt Florrie's second youngest son, Jamie, who puked over the baby in the car that Easter Sunday years ago, trains horses for the National Hunt.

I have not seen Bill for years. He has been abroad, living in the wilds of Arkansas, way beyond Little Rock. Everything is little over there, he tells me as we move from the orchard in a slow procession. We will go to a local hotel for a meal.

"It's the part of America you never get to hear about," he says. I have never been to America. It is pleasant to hear him talk, to be distracted, to imagine the forgotten history that inhabits the present. He talks about artefacts. A knife-handle lost in the sediment of a river, dropped by some fleeing Indian two hundred years ago. In breaks between semesters, he leaves the university at which he teaches Anglo-Irish studies, to spend time in the wilds; on canoes and barges, or simply trekking with his companions for weeks on end.

We chat in a desultory way about the past years. I have never forgotten that afternoon in Tongs Lough. It has rested securely in my personal store of events of significance. Just as Rose had decided she was bowing out of life, there we were, discovering it for all it was worth.

"What're you grinning at?" Sam asks.

"Thinking back — to Bill and me."

Sam tosses his head indifferently, eyeing Bill with a quizzical expression.

At the hotel there are drinks for anybody that wants them. We are famished and my fingers have begun to go numb. Somehow, going out after a burial lightens things; the sweet and dry sherries, the whiskeys and gins are comforting. It seems possible that life can be continued when one is surrounded by people one knows and the aroma of hot food drifts around. We cry in fits and starts.

Chapter Nineteen

—ᏫᏫ—

At the Barra de Brún Gallery women's art is celebrated. Woman revered by woman! Authenticity! A mishmash of the good, the mediocre and the dreadful. There are predictable images, mountains which symbolise breasts, Mother Earth in repose on the landscape. A view of the Hellfire Club in the Dublin Mountains becomes a breast with a nobbly-looking nipple. A piece of fruit represents female genitalia luridly exposed. A vegetable marrow is a vagina.

Further along, there are portraits from a private collection. I move slowly, searching for something which will command me to stop. The atmosphere is churchlike. People whisper, their footsteps muffled by the carpeting. They move with caution, as if afraid of saying or doing the wrong thing. A portrait of a man and a woman catches my attention. It is not what one would expect at an exhibition like this. The textures are rough and it has been worked in oils, not acrylics. A naked man and woman pose at angles to one another. At one point their shoulders touch but otherwise they stare in nearly opposite directions. Her hand covers her mouth. She could be wiping it or concealing it the way people do when they've made a mistake. He frowns, though a smile plays at the corners of his mouth. What is striking about both figures are their huge hands, their coarse golden hair and their elusive expressions. The image says more than all the self-regarding physical appendages can ever say, asserts more about the nature of the human than any earth mother or mountain could possibly do.

I would like to buy it. After all, I'm flush, always a good reason for extravagance. I ask the woman on the desk for a catalogue, run a finger rapidly down the list. It seems hardly possible. Nonetheless it is true. K Troy, *Somebody's Daughter, Somebody's Son*. The picture is not for sale. Excitement rushes through me. This is to meet Kate half a year later and find her alive and well. It is to hear her voice, to listen to her wisdom when least expected. I should recognise her style, but then the picture is not in her usual mould and secondly I am caught off-guard. It is as if her presence bears down on me. A feeling of past affections. The dreaded hair-trigger moment overwhelms me.

"We have to thank the good earth," she said one September when we were very young and she insisted that we dance round the rowan tree in the garden, joining in with us, clasping our hands firmly in hers.

But I am her lost and sorrowing daughter. Kate's death is real, I am inconsolable, would give anything to hear her voice again. The way it used to be. Confident, happy, in control. She was all that I am not, and a foothold at the rim of every disaster.

Chapter Twenty

—⚡︎—

Sam's newest building is underway near the river esplanade on the southside of the city. It will be a magnificent palace, complete with leisure-centre, massage-room and sauna for the lords of commerce who will lease it. Computers, consoles, up-to-the-minute technology, video-facilities for trans-global conferences whereby the participants will not even have to leave their own countries in order to take part; everything, in fact, that holders of power could possibly desire, including exclusive views of the mountains and the sea.

He has never held such a contract, has been given *carte blanche* to produce the design of his dreams. Letters fly to and fro in a hectic round of planning and anticipation as the quantity surveyor, the builders, the engineer and the clerk of works "liaise" with Sam and Tony. Everything is processed in triplicate. Sam has recently added a new piece to his lead crystal collection: a tiny glass house, transparent from every angle, devoid of overt colour, yet inviting concentrations of light at every turn.

In the midst of all this, I try to draw close, to edge him towards communication. I imagine us living in such a glass house. Instead of our eight-inch cavity-blocked walls, we could gaze through wall after wall from any part of the house, following each other, our vision obscured only by the occasional slanting glare of sun. I imagine us at night in our glass bed, revolving outside space and time, our dwelling freed of the limitations of earth, as if we inhabited a glass star in an undiscovered galaxy.

Something niggles at me as he takes down some rolled-up sheets and spreads them on the kitchen table. He is wildly enthusiastic about Sandrine's projections. "This is how she sees the first-floor interior—what proportions! Breakthrough stuff, you know? And just look at those ventilation ducts!"

I do not know what to think. The waxed paper contains fine precise black line-drawings which even now puzzle me, and not because of their concrete intricacies. I have never been able to decipher the mathematics of architecture, that feat of imagination which can translate a schema into a picture. Aware that Sam's attention is trained on the new building, I bend over the sheets to search for some clue. The offices will be large and bright, with reinforced glass and steel cladding the dazzling exterior. His descriptions demand some sort of response from me, this lyrical enthusiasm for the riverside location and all that glass.

"The effect of light on material surrounds can be dramatic," I tell him. It is, after all, the ground matrix on which my own work depends for composition.

"It's going to be very sharp, aesthetically alive too, but subtle. It's all about light really," he replies.

We are talking past one another. Formalities. Empty words damming up what should stream freely.

Days pass. I take the train to the west on Tuesday and tell him not to expect me before Thursday evening. The trip means an unusual expedition to the islands. A group of young, enthusiastic actors have brought their production to people who rarely get to the mainland. It is the kind of idea that sends east-coast editors into a frenzy of enthusiasm, demanding copy to be illustrated by photographs of artists making contact with the noble peasants. I have been sent to accompany the troupe, to capture the essential pictures which will convey the novelty of these island theatricals. My stills will be moody. I favour such images, and on the island there is gorgeous colour, all determined by the sea. Life there has a patina produced by centuries of wind and rain and muck and lichens — a sense of abstract, Celtic mystery.

The production has received so much advance publicity that I feel alienated. It is difficult to avoid prejudice. I dislike being told that I must whoop about something. I despise hyperbole and the hip-hip-hooray tendency still to applaud that which does not always merit applause. In the harbour every *soi-disant* poet and playwright in the country crowds into the boat. The western town is packed with summer tourists. American and German voices rise above the local garble and a few Scandinavians with discreet cameras and sensible rainwear, have joined the little expedition.

The ocean opens before us and the journey is rough. People start to look uneasy, queasiness settling in already. I am an excellent seafarer. On honeymoon with Sam, one day I steered the little boat we had rented back into shore while he sprawled out, splay-legged and green-faced.

My sense of superiority increases as I observe one of the poets, a little leprechaun of a man with a small bottle of Paddy whiskey protruding from his brown jacket pocket, puke vigorously into the sea. Those who stand downwind of his retching hasten to the other side of the boat. Fortunately, roaring gusts whip the rancid odour quickly away, and the poet, not in the least put out, tidies himself up, mopping his beard with a red handkerchief which is drawn in a ball from his other pocket.

The usual crowd are aboard. Media people—tape-recorders at the ready, playboys of the airwaves, the occasional woman poet, all streeling hair and pale skin in the style of the pre-Raphaelites. As ever, I am in two minds about artists, the photographer in me at war with abstractions of words. Nowadays everybody writes.

The poet gives one last retch as the trawler is roped in by a boy standing on the island pier. The ensuing hours pass quickly. I photograph the actors and islanders, cast about for odd angles of light and shadow and for some unposed shots as people mingle and chat. Later, although the evening brightens again, there is a terrific wind from the Atlantic. The actors are sheltered beneath a huge tarpaulin at one of the island's highest points, and perform around old dolmens and bleached trees.

All around, people stand reverently, notebooks and programmes to hand. By the last act of the play, an unlikely Restoration comedy to which the island punters respond with keen and genuine amusement, the wind drops. The ground is damp after the previous day's storm. There is orangey lichen, rough grass, moss. The sunset is flamboyant, yet cold. I take a wide-angle shot of the seascape. Through the camera lens, the world is a rectangle of order and wilderness and the ocean a heaving animal that breathes uneasily, its hide gouged by a spectrum of deepening reds.

As I adjust the camera for one final shot, a mischievous voice whispers in my ear. "Hello stranger!" It's Bill!

"Hello coz," I reply, to cover my surprise. "Should've known you'd be here."

"Naturellement," he replies drolly. "Couldn't miss a spectacle like this." His smirk is collusive, his eyes affectionate.

"Quite good, isn't it?" I egg him on, knowing he'll disagree.

"Tourist blather," he laughs derisively. "It'll lure the Germans out for one night at least." He laughs again, a big-voiced, easy chuckle.

"It's better than I expected," I argue. I want to keep him talking.

"Suppose you're here in your photographer's hat," he drawls, placing a bent cigarette between his teeth.

"Of course. What brought you? Poetic compulsion? Research for your young Anglo-Irish lit. enthusiasts out in Little Rock?"

He shakes his head, smiling at me.

"What then?" I press. "The crack? Haring after some woman?"

He exhales smoke in narrow jets which are instantly dispelled by the wind.

"Something to do. Crack possibly — I'm at a loose end — and I wondered if you might be here."

"Ah."

"Ah," he mimics back.

"Well, here I am," I answer awkwardly, feeling absurdly self-conscious.

Back inside the tarpaulin again, we clap loudly with the audience as the actors bow. Clearly, many of those present thought the production good. There are wolf-whistles and yahoos and cheers. One of the leading actresses draws a third and a fourth ovation from the crowd, timing her fleet-footed exits and modest entrances to perfection. I plan to remain on the island a second night and go back to the coast the following morning to wait for a visiting theatre-company from the south. The whole country is on the move. Just the sort of copy the editor likes. Plenty of newsy clichés. But the slight unease I felt before leaving home has not disappeared; if anything, it is more acute. In the absence of a reason for such anxiety, it is all the more worrying. On impulse, I decide to return home the next day.

A publicity man called Ron hands me an enormous information pack. He is pleasant but I dislike having wet kisses plonked on my cheek. Ron is a great man for the kisses and embraces. At any function he can be seen gliding across the floor towards his prey, arms extended, teeth bared, eyes like stone.

"Let's move, shall we?" I nudge Bill.

The wind has dropped almost completely as we stroll down the rough path towards the narrow road that leads to the village. People tramp downhill in groups, islanders and mainlanders, the night full of good-humoured laughter. We walk carefully, avoiding the dried cowpats and the sharp snagging stones, consciously inhaling the salty funk that wafts up from the shore.

Life with Sam has become compressed, every action and thought tight and unyielding. It is like being squeezed out of your own existence, as if his impenetrability were an expanding organism forcing its way into the mind until it too is pressed tight, like an orange in a fruit-press.

In The Cockle, Bill and I settle into reading the menu. He opts for sole on the bone, I for trout. They arrive served with lots of cress, field mushrooms and green peppers. There are new potatoes in mint and fennel butter. The woman brings us a bottle of Partager red, which we knock back fairly quickly.

"What about your book?" I ask.

"Coming along. I keep getting distracted by other work—lectures and stuff."

"Perhaps that's all to the good."

"Why should it be?" he snaps.

I have trodden on poetic corns. "Because maybe then only the really urgent poems will get written—you know, the ones that matter. Anyway—" I pause to refill my wine-glass, "—it's impossible to gauge the quality of things within the confines of the present."

"But I'm not interested in being discovered after I die," he says morosely. "Lord knows I've enough contacts in the States now, real Hibernophiles."

"Don't you care for immortality then?"

"I don't give a blind fuck about being remembered when I snuff it."

"I was only asking. You're right. Immortality is useless."

"Maybe. Most writers would turn in their graves if they saw what happens to their work after they die," he says huffily.

"Look at Kavanagh and Yeats."

"Exactly. Though Kavanagh wasn't as good as people made out—ignorant gobshite."

"Ah, but weekends and festivals are an industry, you know," I say as we tuck into the meal.

"Art made accessible and relevant?" he queries across his glass. I refill it.

"Art with a capital F is what I say."

He drops his head back and laughs. "Fair play to you, Hanna. Still as awkward as ever, I see."

"Probably," I agree with him.

"You never did suffer fools gladly. Cripes, this fish is good, I was starving!" he rambles. "By the way, how's old Sam keeping?"

"Fine. Fine really." His reference to old Sam rankles slightly.

"What does that mean?"

I shrug my shoulders. "Oh, nothing in particular. Hard to explain. You know Sam."

"Not really. He and I never really hit it off—I mean, there's no rapport."

129

"That's how it goes with in-laws and relatives. If you find one you really like, consider yourself lucky. I avoid Sam's side of the family at certain times, you know how things are—I have to be in top form or else I come away feeling depressed."

"Still, Hanna," Bill brings me back to the point, "you and Sam have stuck it out pretty well. Most couples I know have split up within eight years at the most."

"Yes, well—" I am filled with doubt. "There's more to it than sticking things out."

Outside, the island looks almost Mediterranean by night. A half-hearted loop of coloured lights dangles at the pier, a few white yachts bob unevenly, alongside fine, wooden-shafted trawlers. People stroll by wearing coats and jackets against the June chill. Others pause outside the restaurant and examine the menu. The Americans make lengthy calculations. It has filled up since our arrival, all the side alcoves and most of the centre tables now occupied, and the solitary waitress is at her wits' end trying to deal with everybody. Every so often she screams in the kitchen about that fucker Tomás and why the hell he's never on time; well she'll settle his hash when Herr Schlinger gets back.

"Must be owned by Krauts," I observe.

"Have you booked any place for the night?"

"Not yet."

"There are rooms here."

We look at one another quickly. It is an assessing look which confirms that we are working towards a situation, one that I have occasionally imagined. I do not dare to believe that it will be translated into reality, despite my soul-searching in recent times, especially since the funeral.

"What about here, so?" he suggests, leaning back in his chair and wiping his lips with a napkin. "Would you like that?"

"Yes," I reply, astonished at the swiftness with which things have moved.

"Good. Can't think of anything that would make me happier, that would fill me with such joy, as to share a room, by which of course I mean a bed, with Hanna Troy!"

The presumption does not disturb me in the slightest. It is nothing I have not considered, automatically and heedlessly. I want to prove something to myself, my desirability perhaps, and in the company of someone I can trust.

Herr Schlinger is absent until the weekend, the waitress informs us, but she will take our reservation.

"Single or double—double I suppose?" she asks bluntly and loudly.

We buy another bottle of wine. Bill grumbles about the wine-list. "If this place is owned by a German, how come the list is so abysmal?"

"It's a local restaurant, sir. That's all they'll buy here," she replies, twirling her pencil.

"But you have summer visitors, like us!" he insists. The woman studies him as if trying to establish if he's a crank or whether she should go ahead with the reservation.

"Yes, sir, I'm afraid that's all we have at present—the wine, I mean!" she corrects herself, giggling suddenly.

"Jesus!" I titter when she leaves. "Do you have to go on about the wine so much?"

"Ah, feck it, she got up my nose with her 'Double, I suppose' carry-on. It made me feel like someone on a dirty weekend."

"Guilt."

"No, it's just that it's high time people stopped making a big thing of adults who are obviously not married wanting to share the same room!"

"You have a lot of experience of this, so?" I tease him.

"No. But I hear things."

When she returns with the bedroom key, he is more contrite, has reached over to stroke my hand.

"Thank you," I tell her.

"Will you be wanting early breakfast?" she inquires.

Bill and I hesitate. "No," he answers for both of us.

He continues to stroke my hand, talks about feeling nervous.

"What about? I'm no stranger," I say.

"We're mad – bonkers – you realise that, don't you?"

"I realise it. I've always realised that. And I love it."

For once I do not care about Bill's nervousness, or my own. I have spent my life living carefully and competently. It has proven worthless. I have photographed those who have taken risks, those who abandon themselves for the sake of greatness or self-seeking or for something intangible, those who sail close to the wind, regardless of personal commitment. And I have taken such care with Sam Wright, whom I knew as a boy and have followed into early middle-age. Obviously not the right kind of care, however, and something must happen for both our sakes. I am determined to return tomorrow, regardless of what transpires. We must change in some way. I will not put up with the situation any longer.

Nonetheless I have no desire to change my plans for the night now, will not fudge the prospect of holding Bill in my arms once again. The room is at the top of a twisting wooden staircase, built into the low attic. It is small, clean and functional, with white walls and a print of a Paul Henry landscape. I dither. Supposing he is so nervous that he laughs, not at me, but at nothing in particular, the way I do when I'm really nervous. What if I find him repulsive? We remove our clothing on opposite sides of the narrow double bed with minimal decorum. There are dark bruises on his thighs, the result of injecting himself with insulin. Bill is diabetic and after all the wine we've drunk has to inject himself again. I watch fascinated, desire abated as he jabs himself efficiently.

Things are awkward in bed. There are so many lies about men and women, one of the most idiotic being that the penis is a blunt instrument capable of creating untold delights simply by thrusting. We have overlooked one thing: desire. By the time we are in bed, the whole night has lost its promise. He is more slender than Sam, his skin smoother to touch, shoulders bonier. This is the man who was once the boy who made love with me in Tongs Lough. That is the sole reason we have gone to bed together. We have a foundation based securely in the past and imagine it confers certain rights.

"But have you, do you—often?" My question hangs in the air.

"All the time!" he sings evasively, turning on his side and gazing into my face.

"Seriously?"

"Hardly ever. I don't think I ever made the earth move for any woman—Lord knows I've had enough trouble making it move for myself."

"Funny that."

"Odd, you might say, but not funny. The old libido isn't—well—I'm no Rambo."

"Well, bully for you then! Who the hell wants the nearest thing to a piece of beef in bed with them?"

"You'd be surprised what women want. You're one. You should know, Hanna."

"Do we scare you a bit?"

He rolls onto his back to consider, starts to say something but decides not to.

"Perhaps. A little. Men's company is easier."

Eventually we sleep, back to back but not touching. It has been a non-event. Nothing works deeply on me any more. Bill has grown to be an exceptionally nice intellectual and poet. Well-adjusted as they go.

Chapter Twenty-One

—ⱳ—

In the light of morning I no longer want to be with Bill but
am anxious to be up and about and on my way back to the
city. He lies inert, his lashes twitching slightly. I dress quietly,
scribble a quick note and slip away. There will be a boat by
seven fifteen and the sea is calm. Tired as I am, my sense of
anticipation outweighs any guilt I might feel, and I am ready
to take on whatever might come my way that day. My hair is
unkempt, my clothes—a red knitted sweater, loose wool skirt
and blue plastic cape—creased and rumpled. But the camera-
bag feels light on my shoulder.

It is as if, by leaving those dreamy, mist-wreathed
mountains that slope to the sea, I can return afresh. If I
simply banish Bill from my head and refuse to dwell on
the events of the previous night, I can convince myself
that nothing really happened, which is more or less
the truth anyway. What do I hope for? We pass through
village stations where geraniums struggle in pots and
weedy flowers grow from makeshift urns which are really
old tractor tyres painted white. People bid one another
goodbye: an awkward squeeze here, a quick, embarrassed
peck on the cheek there. Despite such offhandedness,
they are saying *I love you*. Through it all, the person left
behind struggles to retain composure as the train pulls out.

Mothers. Aunts. An old farmer whose pert dark-haired daughter can hardly wait to get shot of him.

I hope that in my absence something might have changed, that Sam will have experienced some revelation and greet me with enthusiasm. The train chugs across the midlands, through stone-walled fields, past crops of barley, then into the black stretches of bog where birches and mountain-ash bend to the wind. I think back to the weekend when Kate and Dan visited, how bloodily we made love. Hunger, that is the thing. To know that appetites have been whetted, that there is a surging vitality for something, anything. I will try again. I am afraid to live without Sam.

Somewhere at the back of my mind I believe in our hunger, what is uniquely ours. But it recedes with every week. I have grown a hard outer shell. What lies within is a mystery even to me. The tides of my body leave me distraught these days. Every month is the same. I fill up. My breasts swell, my stomach grows heavy. How magnificent to be a woman on the brink of bleeding! The life that flows through my being! I smell different. Warmer, sweeter, even to myself, my breasts demand more attention, every curve is fuller, more sloping; I ought to be admired. Those few short hours before it begins make me invincible. But then it starts and rushes from me in a matter of days, leaving a dried-up old pod, empty receptacle, the sense of receding tides. I am never so barren as in the days after. In any other language the word *dry* has a more explicit, rustling sound. Words like *sèche* and *secco*, *trocken* and *tirim*. I am old leaves, brown and sere, swept to the hollows.

A woman in the seat opposite watches me. We are playing a game in the carriage window. Who will catch whom looking in the glass? Determined not to meet her eye, I bore through her image to the rushing hedgerows outside, study meadow flowers with globes and knots of purple and pink, watch for

135

summer birds frightened by the train. On the other side of the corridor a nun reads her breviary. Nuns are a safe bet on trains. The female traveller's rule of thumb: sit near one and you won't be bothered by drunks or creeps.

By the time the train pulls into the station I am inexplicably fearful again. Sam may well be home. I will be bright and cheerful and we shall recover something of our former momentum. That momentum has never been light. Lightness of mood has never characterised Sam's life. I head through the crowds for the carpark. It is raining. All the way east we have headed into cloud, leaving the West calm and sunny. I will develop the stills later, when the darkrooms are freer and the newsroom is quiet.

Unusually, Sam's car is parked out on the road. Normally he leaves it close to the house but today it blocks the drive and I cannot get in. Pulling up behind his Morris Minor, I survey the house swiftly and notice that he's forgotten to open the bedroom curtains and that the downstairs windows are open. Moreover, the bathroom window at the side of the house is wide open. Steam billows out; Sam is showering and I decide to surprise him, begin to pull at my sweater the moment I shut the hall door quietly and to undo the buttons of my skirt. Then I stop, rooted. I hear voices, drop my camera-bag stealthily, a sense of dread swelling, billowing within me.

I stand there too long. They have stumbled uproariously from the bathroom, presumably towards our bedroom. Even downstairs, the air is warm and damp with steam. They roar their heads off. Sandrine's voice sounds crude and vulgar. The laughter would be intoxicating were it not for the fact that the situation is occurring in my own home, that one of the chief participants is Sam. For a split second I too want to participate, feel every right to join in and laugh with them.

136

Yet my mouth is dry. I will awaken to discover a bad dream. There is relative calm for a while. I consider that perhaps I have hallucinated, that my guilt about sleeping with Bill the previous night is perhaps greater than I have admitted.

Never conceal beyond what is prudent, Kate once told me and Rose, on one of those occasions when Rose admitted to having an affair with a married man. In a way, she was telling us to have our cake and eat it. We were walking on a beach. She moved with strength in her limbs, stronger in build than either Rose or me, though both of us were taller. She stripped nimbly, uninhibited by the presence of families who clustered between rocks. We swam together, cutting the water with confidence. Then she slipped over into a slow, lazy backstroke. Unconsciously, I did the same. High above me a seagull hovered, screaming. Sunlight silvered its belly. The sky was a perfect blue and the water a bearable temperature. I was flooded with happiness in that moment, knew my place in the scheme of things. I imagined Kate going on for ever, becoming part of the earth, the universe. We would all inhabit that earth. I yearned to swim on and out then, with Kate, never stopping, animating the world with our blessings, our brilliant happiness.

As the cacophonies of arousal begin, I wonder how long Sam has been concealing the affair, how long has his prudence and circumspection prevented my discovering what was happening right under my nose? Sandrine's voice is wild and desperate, as if she is drowning, as if she needs more and more air and cannot get enough. As if she is going to die unless something happens. Sam is noisy too, as he has never sounded with me. The mounting passion. The excitement. The sheer, fully-sexed abandon. Bill and I are mere babes in the wood in comparison.

"Oh Sandrine, Sandrine," he moans.

What is he doing? I have to know what is happening. Have to see this episode or dream or whatever it is through to the end. The yowling mounts. The grunts become rhythmic. Soon they are in unison. Then a long drawn-out howl as she screams out of some sort of extended, intense pleasure. A mystery surely. This cannot be Sam's doing.

My stealth surprises me as I move upstairs, up and around the long spiral that leads to the landing. If this were a film, the heroine would burst in and either shoot the miscreants or exchange withering looks before turning on her heel to make a dignified exit. Instead, I approach the bedroom on tiptoe. The door is ajar. I risk the occasional glimpse, then pull back as if my face had been branded by flames. He is rolling her around our bed, the very bed we chose with such painstaking care years ago, so that it would be long enough, wide enough and very firm. I am oddly excited by the spectacle, as if it were a slow-motion film-noir experiment with light and shadow, as if the pair of them awaited the art of my camera to cast its magnificent eye on the sequence of events.

She is on top of him. All I can see is her back, and the little nodules of her spine as she grinds forwards and back on his pelvis. The whimpering begins again. Sam is with her all the way. When they have satisfied themselves, he draws her up beneath him, spreads her knees, pushing her head and shoulders well down, and enters her from behind. I observe her creamy flanks. He knows what he's doing, has not come fresh to this experience. The last thing I see is Sam turning her around, opening her legs and burying his head, his mouth, his entire face.

Downstairs again, I have no plan. It is as if my physical body has dissolved. Their voices rise. He sounds tender and considerate, and they have begun to laugh yet again. Life is a wonderful joke shared between lovers.

Again, the screeching and howling, as if they were demented. Such sounds are something I have neither imagined nor experienced. I pull the front door quietly and go to the car. It starts smoothly. It could so easily have seized up and then I would have had to remain trapped with them, would have to confront them. My hands are cold and wet, my head pounds. Sam has obviously installed Sandrine for the duration of the afternoon at least, and in all probability for the night. I will not spray them with lead. Nor will I set fire to the house. I will proceed calmly to the best hotel I can find and pass the evening in comfort. There I will consider my next move. I do not know if this is the end. The very least is that I shall be doing my thinking in some civilised environment.

The hotel is a modern edifice, near the waterfront.

"How long will you be staying?" the receptionist asks.

I notice her nails. Polished and filed, like little red claws. Her mouth is pinked-up, her make-up flawless.

"One night."

"Do you have some identification?"

I open my bag slowly and produce a Bibliotheque Franchise reader's card.

"Room four-oh-four, madam," she says efficiently, handing me a smooth key with a large plastic tag attached.

The bed is firm and springy, the linen fresh. There is a small tea-maker in one corner. The furnishings are comfortable, with fussy curtaining and an arching canopy over the bed in rich greens and blues. My head hurts and I feel ill. I pace up and down. Bitterness builds. The need to scream, to do violence.

I lift the phone and dial Anna's number. There is no answer, which is just as well. For an instant I consider calling Tony. But what does one say to a man who is probably up to his eyes in work, at the office on a Wednesday evening? Finally, I light on Rose. Erkus answers.

"Is Rose there?"

"Who's that?"

"Hanna."

"Oh. Didn't recognise you for a minute. Hang on." The phone is clunked down. I hear footsteps as Rose approaches.

"Hi," she says lightly.

"Hi. Just thought I'd give you a bell."

But it is a mistake. Rose sounds preoccupied and remote.

"Any news?" she asks casually. I hear her drum her fingers on the table, the way she used to at home.

"Just got in from a shoot in the West," I mutter. "Look, if you're busy I can call again, okay?"

"Well, as a matter of fact we do have some people here right now," she whispers. "Awfully nice people, I'll fill you in next time."

"No problem."

"You'll have to meet them when we get together."

"Okay, well — I'll be in touch then," I say, without waiting for her to say goodbye.

In the bathroom, I take my time squeezing a long layer of red and white toothpaste on the brush, spend some minutes scrubbing and rinsing, scrubbing and rinsing as if to wash away the vile taste of my existence. I examine all the little packages of bathroom gels and creams, the scented phials, the soft bathrobes (two, the hotel didn't have a single room) in pink and green. As I turn, my elbow catches a drinking-glass, and it crashes to the floor. A sliver lodges in my stockinged foot. I watch the small trickle of blood and drop to my hunkers to remove the glass, crouch there for ages, hands around knees, squatting beneath the sink, an intolerable pain dredging my chest.

Chapter Twenty-Two

—ᴍ—

None of the pictures is for sale. The gallery attendant is officious, one of those intellectual types, asexual in dress, all faint smiles and superiority. I try to persuade her to let me have the name and address of the painting's owner. When I say I'm Kate Troy's daughter, she looks at me, doubt in her grey eyes.

Now I understand why people turn on great works of art and slash them to pieces. I know why that guy laid into the Pieta with a hammer years back and why another chap ripped into a Van Gogh. They were not believed in. Nobody told those poor bastards that their lives were worth a damn, and so the only way they could get a response, even an outraged one, was to defile a revered object.

In that moment I know the secret thrill of sacrilege, destruction; know why people smash tabernacles and holy objects. I do not want to touch Kate's painting but as I turn on my heel, I want to shove the attendant's head through one of the other portraits.

The junction between Nassau Street and Dawson Street is clogged with traffic and people. Am I the only woman on the lower reaches of middle-age, stuck ludicrously between these confident youngsters and the sludge-paced American tourists? Tour buses line the street, opposite the row of shops which display the kind of authentic Irish ware that some whizz-kid dreamed up as a commercial joke in the seventies. We're a nation of potters and glazers; every home had terracotta flowerpots for most of this century. There were certainly no pigs in the kitchen or, if there were, they were of the ornamental variety — cheap, glazed, porcine delph. The wheels of commerce turn and turn. On Nassau Street I can practically hear them humming. We will claim anything to be authentically ours if it guarantees a fast return and an image acceptable to the rest of Europe.

There's no escaping some things. I drift through bookshops further up Dawson Street. Books have never been so popular. The men and women who browse casually are frequently desperate to secure something for themselves from life. We strike bargains all the time. There's an unwritten understanding between us and life which hints that if we put up with all the nastiness that slaps us in the face then we're entitled to some happiness. We're owed something.

A lot of people swallow that but I've long ago given up. Life owes me nothing, even though I'm so angry I'd like to kick the shit out of it. I wander up to the first floor. The more specialised stuff is always that bit out of reach.

I almost falter as I spot the book: the banned one that has finally been released on the Irish market. A sex manual, the most explicit going, all in the best *possible* taste, according to its author. A number of others hover in the vicinity. The sex manuals are shelved between R for *Rock-Climbing* and T for *Tantra*. One man removes a rock-climbers' guide. He is slimly built, wears plus-fours and carries a small knapsack on one shoulder. To my right a young woman thoughtfully turns the pages of a book on meditation. I reach up and remove the sex manual; I will not be shamed into buying it without first having a decent look. Not for the first time, I question our sexual proclivities. Mine and Sam's. Nothing extraordinary, nothing out of the way. Enjoyable as far as I was concerned. But Sam has been less than satisfied, although he claims that sex has nothing to do with it. That is what all men say when they are in the middle of an intensely sexual liaison with somebody else. The drawings in the book are discreet to the point of monotony. Line-drawings, poorly etched. The expression of the partners is bland. They sure don't look as if they're having a hectic time, even if they're doing things called Buttered Bun, Doughnut Surprise and Dolphins' Delight.

Never one to be daunted, I buy a copy and leave it with the assistant while I browse. I have a horror of being accused of shoplifting, never choose an item without first leaving it with someone in charge. I return to the section. The man and woman have now homed in on S too, both of them engrossed. She flicks with forced indifference through *What Men Really Want*, he tucks into the *Shere Hite Report*. The book on pregnancy falls open at a chapter headed *Complications of Early Pregnancy*. Then the word practically leaps out, the way important words do when for some reason you've had to absorb them. My eyes glide rapidly through a few paragraphs. I am curious. I need more information to establish some certainty.

Chapter Twenty-Three

—ɯ—

Rose and Erkus sound delirious. They break the news at a party. The place is packed with people I do not know. I am not in the mood for gaiety but Rose has asked me to come. I make excuses for Sam.

"We've got news," she gushes down the phone.

I have a fair idea of its nature even before heading out the coast road. A long clutter of cars and motorbikes trails on both sides of the road and down towards the cliff. One vehicle moves rhythmically from side to side and its windows are steamed up. The windows of the cottage are flung wide and I recognise the sound of Genesis. Not my thing. The few years between Rose and me mean that our musical tastes are completely different, yet it was she who later recognised U2's potential. It is Rose who composes memorable chants to be sung on "Reclaim the Night" marches through the city.

She is a woman of her time, for all times. We, who come from the most benign of backgrounds, have occasionally discovered sisterhood through the traumas of others. We have not been molested by our father, nor raped by our uncles, nor beaten, nor abused in the reported modern way. That she has a tendency to physical self-abuse is a particular private kink. Yet Rose is part of a team of telephone Samaritans who deal with calls from the frantic and the lonely. I would

144

trust her with any secret, at any time, and know that in her funny, untidy way she would provide reliable advice on any problem.

As usual at Rose and Erkus's parties, there's home-made plonk and fruit juices in abundance, cherry juice, fizzies and gallons of tar-like coffee to go with the pizzas they live on. Many of their friends are reformed drug-addicts. The party is like a recovery session. People sit around in groups and a good deal of soul-baring takes place in between heavy work-outs to the music. The smoke—they all smoke, without exception—is thick and the place stinks.

I regard my older sister with renewed interest. Years ago I stopped telling her things when it became clear that she never listened anyway. Then we began to talk on the marches and sometimes on the phone. Rose is a marvellous telephone person, her voice intimate and confiding as she relates or advises according to the demands of the moment. Tonight her eyes sparkle; Erkus holds her close. There's a lot of back-slapping and toasting to them both and to the future. She's pregnant. I am not surprised. She has often spoken of the possibility, about having a child with Erkus.

"Have you told Dan?"

"We phoned today and gave him the good news."

"Well?"

"He was just delighted; he couldn't believe it—he can hardly wait to see us." She pauses to light a cigarette. "I think probably he was a bit confused at first—you know Dan—but he's simply amazing when it comes to things like this!"

"He is?" This is news to me but I am not about to burst Rose's bubble.

I know Dan. Rose is naive enough to imagine that he is pleased at the news. She is equally selfish enough not to have considered that at his age the whole thing might be a bit

145

rich. Dan has never admired the wanton gesture, despite his tolerance of foibles.

I push my way through the room, searching for a familiar face. We have always moved in different circles. She is gregarious and surrounds herself with bright, talkative people. I can be gregarious but usually am circumspect and cautious, rather like Sam. Shy is another word for it. I have an innate distrust of those who equate noise with fun. Rose has become a city person if ever there was one and could move easily in any metropolitan circle. She has lived in New York, London and Berlin, has acted in two-bit plays off-off-Broadway and never conceals her loathing of press people like me.

"Parasites," she used to say, rather unoriginally I thought.

A sense of dislocation pervades the cottage that night. Part of me, a great part, wants to go back home. To our first home. There's something forgotten, something lost sight of. I think back to the Sundays and family gatherings with Kate and Dan and the Bardons and Binchys and I am perplexed. Bill fitted in somewhere too. Now he seems discontent. There was something solid about those years in Clonfoy, as if what was real back then held more substance than reality does today. But perhaps that is just one more illusion, part of the process of time passing, the discovery of imprisoning kinds of maturity.

And home could be boring too. Who doesn't find parents and home crucifying at times? Think of the Sunday afternoons when there are no outings planned. People sprawl beneath half-read newspapers, the house smells of gravy and dinner, the dog snores, the fire crackles with cindery wood and outside the damp seeps into the whole world. I recall the saturating boredom, the desire to be elsewhere doing something interesting, to be strolling down some boulevard, living with a hippy and making wild, passionate love every night and between meals. But I was reined in, hemmed in on every side. Even Kate's advice could be stifling, despite its wisdom; it came too close at times to inhibiting our capacity to choose. Rose probably felt this more acutely than I did, being the eldest. Probably it was she who first experienced Dan and Kate's sensible streak, their united front on matters educational.

"If you have your education and a good career, then you can do what you like," Kate would say. "Look at me, dependent on your father for everything, not that I mind, but all the same...If he was a different kind of man, it mightn't be so cosy."

I wonder what she'd think of us now, what *did* she think of us before she died?

Erkus moves to the centre of the room, dragging Rose by the arm. I cannot seriously believe that she is reluctant, that she is doing anything more than going through the motions of playing shy. Their sitting-room is full of fashionable junk. Not for Rose the Laura Ashley or Sanderson look. This is white-walled mock simplicity—bodhrans and flutes. They both play them after a fashion as part of their various morning meditations. They don't bother with curtains as such but hang heavy woollen blankets from hooks, drape ethnic rugs here and there, throw large swathes of crimson silk material over tables. It is a mixture of the old and the crudely fashioned and I like it, wish I shared Rose's touch when it comes to creating physical surrounds. I've left a lot of that up to Sam, indulged his penchant for experimenting with space and light, lived on the whole content with his ideas about the house.

"Well, folks, you know us," Erkus begins breathlessly.

A string of mauve stones hangs from his neck. He is

147

braceleted with more stones and wears an oval of black onyx on his right forefinger.

"The news of the night, the news of my life—O God, it's so amazing I can hardly believe it!" he gasps, "—is that Rose and I are—*pregnant.*"

Everybody whoops and cheers. It's like the Muppet Show, with a great deal of jiggling and prancing and head-nodding. The two dogs bark like mad; then poke their long snouts into the hands of anybody willing to pay them attention. Bringing forth a child is a hip thing among Rose's supporters. Despite my drear mood, I am as enthusiastic as anybody. There's one thing about my sister and her men: they can create an atmosphere, a mood, with ease and confidence. They know how to celebrate—something Sam and I lost the knack of doing. At least I'll be an auntie, I tell myself grimly. The family will go on. There will be continuity. That excites me. Some part of us, of the Troys, will pass on and carry all our strengths and oddities into the future. I beam as I toast them. It's the next best thing to being pregnant myself.

Erkus, naturally, gets carried away. It has all come together for them, he says; they've found one another, found this wonderful home, he's got the shop, Rose isn't doing too bad either, she's just joined this new group and by God are they going to be big, big, big. He sounds like Burt Lancaster in the film *Elmer Gantry*, fists raised in triumph as he spurs his followers on towards the light of discovery, and Rose is with him all the way.

"Right on!" someone calls, striking the air with a mittened fist, and the others nod their heads in approval, pour some more cherry juice or coffee, or light up cheroots.

"Yessir, the light of God is pouring on our heads. I've found Rose, I've found work that I like, sold a parakeet today, ten hamsters, with an order for a boa constrictor, I have a home and now this! My life is complete, I just don't know why this has happened or why I should deserve it but somebody up there must love us!"

His eyes are moist with tears and Rose blinks emotionally. Everybody claps.

"Help yourselves people!" she chirrups, turning away to recover her poise. "There's lots of snacks and dips in the kitchen—Erkie darling, put on the coffee." I follow her into the kitchen. She is dressed in black crushed velvet, with small satin red roses meshed through her hair.

"How does it feel?" I ask, placing my arm round her shoulders. I feel oddly protective. Though younger, I am taller and bigger in every respect. Rose takes after her blood mother and her tallness is balanced by fine bones and marked elegance.

"Magical. Amazing! I just can't believe it, I thought it wasn't going to happen, you know—not at my age."

"Nonsense. Look at those film stars that have them well into their forties—now I *know* what you're going to say, Rose—they can afford it and so on—but it just goes to show: most women can have them well into their forties."

"You're right." She lights another cigarette, then stubs it out guiltily. "I keep forgetting about the ciggies! All the same I feel amazingly lucky. Who would have thought it?" She turns as though something strikes her. "What about you? How do you feel about it—I mean, y'know, the way things are..."

"I feel fine about it," I assure her, "I couldn't be more delighted." I am accustomed to the newly pregnant inspecting me for signs of distress or envy. "What will you do when it's born?"

"Recover!" she laughs, tossing her head as she adds a spoonful of curry-powder to one of her dressings.

"I mean apart from that—what will you do about work?"

"Don't know yet—haven't thought about it—I mean, I've waited long enough for this to happen." She is vague and self-absorbed.

It's difficult to imagine Rose getting up a couple of times a night to mix bottles and feeds but then every woman considers that prospect an impossible one before she actually has to get on with the task. What I really want to know I dare not ask. Deep down I find it hard to believe that Rose will cope. It is nearly always the woman's responsibility, despite all the New Men wandering around the country at present doing unusual things with their hair. What every New Woman knows is that a lot of New Men are there under false pretences. They're masqueraders who call themselves feminists and get away with blue murder. Only true-blue male feminists come through the years of caring for an infant with intact credentials. The poseurs and theorists fall by the wayside, leaving the woman to carry on because a woman will endure under most circumstances, for the sake of the child.

"It'll be great for you all the same," I say acquiescently, thinking that the upheaval will be enormous, almost unimaginable.

At one in the morning I leave the cottage and drive back towards the city. All along the coast, the lights of streetlamps and homes flicker in the dark. There is no fog. I pull into a hotel carpark close to the water's edge and sit looking out. Sam doesn't know that I saw them in bed together. At least he pretends nothing is amiss and made no comment when I moved out into the spare room. I am unable to confront him, fear the consequences, have grown too hardened and yet stay raw.

Sam will leave me. The words must be uttered aloud. *Sam will leave*, I say, sitting in the car with the window wound down. The salty sea smell is calming. Lights are flicked on and off in the hotel bedrooms off to my left. I do not feel maddened. Bereft, yes, but things are manageable. I'm not the first and I won't be the last. There are other fish. Let the ocean have them; let it take all the men I might have loved, who might have been as obtuse as Sam and let it drown them.

Everybody who has ever taken the boat from Dun Laoghaire has memory association that recurs whenever they see the city lights. Mine is of a time when I was sixteen. We are a group of schoolgirls, off on our first trip abroad: destination Amsterdam, by boat and train. As the boat pulls out we jostle one another, all the time watching the fairy lights of Dublin. That night is very beautiful, with mountains falling towards the shores to the south and mystery beyond in the western skyline. We are so certain that we are bound for something more exciting. My passport and money are in the bag Kate bought me for the journey. The giddy pushing and shrieking continues as the boat drones heavily out, well beyond the arms of the harbour. I wave the bag in the breeze, almost drop it into the foam below, passport and all.

A lone trawler bobs quite close to the shore below the cliff. Three men on board, all in sou'westers. The motor is audible, they are probably heading for Dalkey or the Bull Wall.

Happy days.

Daniel goes crazy because they're not married. The fact that Rose is a grown woman in her early forties is beside the point.

But the first sign of something wrong is a telephone call from Erkus.

"The doctor says she's threatening to miscarry."

"What else did he say?"

"Just that, and to take it easy for ten days or so."

"Will they scan her?"

"When the bleeding stops."

"Try not to worry too much," I tell him but the news is not reassuring. I've been listening to Dan grumbling down the phone every day.

"The bloody hound! If I could lay my hands on him!" or "They're not married and that buck can just up and off at the first sign of trouble, leave Rose high and dry!"

"I should think that's most unlikely," I reason.

"You never know—he's a quare hawk, him and his *tonsure*."

He spits out the last word and hangs up with a *humph* sound, reminding me of the camel in Kipling's story. I have not the heart to tell him that what he really can't stand is the prospect of a man knocking up his elder daughter, the fact of their cohabitation and this latest evidence of their activities in what Rose herself would call the "games room."

Dan need not have worried. Next thing Erkus comes on the phone again. I've just put my feet up, in the process of wondering whether or not to phone Anna and suggest a discreet meeting in Bewley's or one of those restaurants where women sort things out.

"She's in hospital."

"What's wrong now?"

"It's an ectopic." *Ectopic*, I mouth to Sam, who sits opposite me with a questioning expression on his face.

Erkus has spent the last hours cleaning up their bedroom. The bed and mattress are ruined, the floor blood spattered.

"I could do nothing except run between the fridge and the bedroom with ice in the hope it'd stop." His voice quivers. "The doctor took ages getting over." I have to drag any further information from him. He is too upset. She's in the operating theatre. She has been in great pain. Her life is not in danger.

152

"Ask him if he wants to come over here," Sam says in a low voice. I shake my head in acknowledgement.

"Will she be all right?" I ask timidly. Deep down I know that Rose will survive this.

"Oh sure, but it's going to be tough on her."

"Jesus," I mutter.

"We were so full of it."

"You were." I pause. "By the way, Sam says to tell you you're more than welcome if you want to spend the night here."

"Thanks. There's no point." He sighs. "I had my suspicions all along. I told her to cool it but there was no talking to her. She was pregnant and she was going to have this baby and that was all there was to it."

At the hospital Rose is groggy. Two days have passed before visitors are allowed. It was more complicated than anybody expected. The surgeon is a woman. The other tube was mucked about but she has managed to save it. Anybody else might have whipped it out.

Rose is white-faced, lies curled up back to the window. When she sees me, she turns her head in response. The air is dry and stuffy with the mixed hospital odours of flowers and rubber mattresses and kitchen smells. Her eyes are puffy, and purple crescents cut into her cheeks. For once I feel the elder: I have been through this hopelessness.

"Tough luck, kiddo," I say.

She stirs and pulls herself up stiffly. "Every move hurts."

The bed is surrounded by flowers and greeting cards. In times of trouble Rose rallies the groups. My niggardly, ungenerous nature takes all this in, because if the tables were turned and it was me in that bed, I feel certain that there would be fewer flowers. I do not attract numbers of jolly well-wishers and supporters, have never had the requisite

153

flamboyance or even, perhaps, the human touch. We talk for a good half-hour before five of her friends arrive, their arms full of flowers and sweetmeats. I am glad she is not alone. There will be enough private recriminations later on. Let her suck in what kindness she can right now.

That evening Dan snivels down the phone to me. Erkus has already broken the news. Despite all his reservations, his resistance to the notion of Rose's pregnancy, this affects him more as it finally strikes him that she and Erkus are living in a state of grief, at least for the moment.

"She's a poor, confused woman," he says with a sigh.

So am I, I feel like screaming. Maybe I'm a poor, confused woman too. My pride forbids them knowing about Sam and Sandrine. I am seen as the capable one, after all, the confident, competent younger daughter who has inherited a fair deal of savvy from her parents.

Now there are two of us, I have a companion in my half-sister but wish this once that our new companionship had a more satisfying foundation. We are panda-bears, the two of us. On the way out. When we die, that will be the end of our branch of the Troys, and all our experiences and thoughts and memories will be filtered out into nothingness. It is unlikely that Rose will conceive now. So the doctor says.

How I wish I could go back and grasp life more fully with Sam, two-handed and lusciously! I know I could compromise, if he would only acknowledge his own quiet loins, admit that he cannot father a child. We could both say, what of it? I could live easily with him, in that imagined glass house, were it not for that failure of admission which in some way deflects a further failure onto me. We could sleep spine to spine, no longer fossils in our imagined lives, but breathing, bathed in light even in the night.

What's life if it cannot be lived? What is time if we cannot aspire to more than flogging each other to death, if we cannot live through it conscious and aware to our fullest capacity? There is only so much we can reach, but what there is, let us have; let us hold it, feel it throb at the centre of our lives.

Chapter Twenty-Four

—⟋m⟍—

Sam's late nights no longer fool me and whether or not he is working it can now be assumed that some of that time is spent, in one way or another, with Sandrine. I am unable to confront him with what I saw and heard after my premature home-coming, finding myself for the first time in my life completely speechless.

Now that the foundations for the new building have been laid, he decides that we should take a holiday. Desperate to find a middle way, I agree. Peace and quiet, release from the work scene, have never seemed more appealing. Sam's company is hardly the most desirable. Yet things *might* sort themselves out at a remove from the familiar.

We book nineteen days in Egypt. He is polite, consulting me as always.

"You don't think it's too long?"

"It might be but we don't have to tour madly."

He is munching a bowl of cereal and gesticulates with the spoon before bringing it to his mouth. I wonder when Sandrine last kissed that mouth.

"We need time. A rest."

He regards me penetratingly. "Are you very tired? You look a little—"

"A little—?" I press as he searches for the word.

His lower lip juts up over his top lip as he considers. "Fatigued. Without colour, I suppose." He, on the other hand, has never looked better. He has spent more time in the open of late, gardening and buzzing around building-sites. He has planted sweet potatoes, beetroot and purple cabbages. The garlic, he claims, is a triumph of traditional wisdom over modern pragmatism. Because he planted the cloves in a circle, the entire bulb is larger than ever, more pungent and without the slightest trace of mould.

"All these things are related, even down to the smallest particle of matter. There's a consciousness of interaction," he lectures out loud one evening, strutting around with a few newly-picked bulbs of garlic in one hand.

The thing with Sandrine is obviously doing wonders for his ego. I oscillate between burning hatred for her, calling down the black plague, and for him murderous feelings mixed with desire.

The flight to Cairo is delayed at Heathrow. The decision to go to Egypt is based, superficially at least, on simple curiosity, which is probably the best reason of all. We wander around the terminal watching flight-screens flicker information. The place is crammed with holidaymakers. Irate foreigners lumber around with loaded trolleys. The shops are packed with bargain-hunters, drifters, big-bottomed Americans. I have both passports and Sam holds the tickets.

Once airborne, we flick through the morning papers in silence, yet our eyes are drawn continuously to the sight beyond the window. Behind us two men argue about the consequences of the Falklands War and how right Maggie was to chastise what they call "Eire" for not backing her. And of course the Irish have to go and call it the Malvinas and back the Argies all the way. It's a civilised discussion but each wants to have the last word.

Stewardesses bustle up and down the aisle. The clink of ice and the gentle, generous glugging of gin into glasses enhances my relief at being away. I repeat the words mentally. *Away! Away!* It's just possible that there's a chance for us, that we might stop floundering. That I love Sam and cannot unlove him is a fact. Is he worth it? The lines between dependency and adult responsiveness blur as always. Impossible to say where one begins and the other ends. Nor is dependency the shameful affliction, the yuppie social disease which everyone wants to avoid. Like a virus, it infects us all to some degree. How we control it is another matter. I have failed, I have failed, I have failed most grievously.

Sam plugs his ears and swallows as we approach Cairo airport. It is evening and the city is spread below like a dusky diamante cloth. Finally the plane bumps and trundles to earth, the tyres smoke as the air-brakes are applied and we roar up the runway towards the terminal.

"At Abu Simbel everybody claps when the pilot makes a successful landing," one of the men behind comments. Sam and I exchange looks and burst out laughing. I take his hand, animosities temporarily dispersed. Already, things are coming right.

The moment we step on to the tarmac, the heat breaks on our faces like a warm wave. It is soothing; the air sweetly wafts Bougainvillaea and sweet tobacco. Brown-skinned, dark-eyed immigration officers eye us casually as they check passports.

Half an hour later we're hurled through the Egyptian night by bus, northwest through Tanta and Damanhur, to Alexandria. There is no air-conditioning and we begin to sweat. We are thirsty and tired. A less familiar companionability has developed between us. I lean back against his arm, he rests his chin against the top of my head. I wonder if anybody would take us to be a honeymoon couple. He is with me and not her. It is like a mantra which must be repeated frequently for maximum benefit. Kate used to say that there were plenty of fish in the sea, especially as she grew older and more petulant. It was usually her parting salvo in any conversation involving troublesome men. Equally, she was likely to remind me that I had made my bed and had better lie on it, all the spoilt caprice of an old, adored woman surfacing prior to her illness. The old sometimes envy the young. They are jealous of young people's optimum independence, the gradual assumption of control that sharpens the pain of their own decline.

Our hotel lies outside the city centre, near the beach. It is a four-storey block in Mandara, and we hurry from the bus, keen to get to our room. Young men in fezzes move briskly, grab cases and bits of luggage, their faces keen and alert. We throw ourselves on the beds in the room and fall asleep quickly with the windows open. The last thing I remember is the sight of white muslin curtains drifting in the light breeze, the quiet scratching sound as they move along the tiled floor, and the ornate wood of the wardrobe doors. Everything smells different; there are hints of aromatic smoke, a spiciness which seems deeply absorbed within every object. Voices rise from the boulevard below and in the distance the rumble of drums rises and falls.

At first the days pass slowly, as if we've been in Alexandria for ever. But this is not the Alexandria of the dead writers, of Durrell and Cafavy, and it is now as modern as it is ancient. The usual beach novelties and cruelties vie for attention. The sand is pinkish. It is a coral beach and people snorkel not far from the shore in order to observe the colours beneath the surface. I read lazily while Sam wanders up and down the seafront examining things. Lion cubs are carted along the beach by photographers. They swing the cats casually, by one paw. The animals make no protest, half-drugged and sleepy.

At other times camels proceed up and down; they bark drily and are often accompanied by baby camels which diligently follow the mothers all day in the trek to and fro.

I buy a snorkel, a mask and a pair of flippers. Sam will not venture into the water, will not swim, no matter what the temperature. Some thirty-five feet from the shore I catch sight of the coral beneath. It takes a while to adjust to using a snorkel. I scarcely trust it but it works. I can breathe and see the world beneath the water. With the slightest twitch of my feet, I am suspended. A whole world lies curled in on itself, struck opaquely by sunlight, wavering and enticing. The formations are like brain images. Everything is convoluted, subtly coloured, and seems to breathe and undulate in slow motion.

Every evening we move out into the city streets and wander through the Corniche. The eastern harbour beside us is spoked with the mastheads of white yachts, the water languid and turquoise. Further in, the air is warm and dusty. We have both been coughing since our arrival: the fine desert sand that blows on the wind causing sniffles and throat-clearing. We are brown by now, fully absorbed by the babble of the Middle East, distracted from ourselves.

We wander through markets past sacks of spice and seed, mounds of chillies, pomegranates, artichokes, fascinated by the haggling and bartering. There are acrobats, organ-grinders, musicians weaving exotic melodies and vigorous drummers. A capuchin monkey perches on the shoulder of a stocky man who plays some kind of flute. It watches the passers-by with pale orange-ringed eyes, its tiny hands thrusting out a plastic box. At other times children accompany the musicians, primed to call the password *Baksheesh*! to passing tourists. Women wearing traditional *haiks* sit in a row in a thick-walled narrow sidestreet to chat and observe. From a distance I wave at them

160

and raise the camera to my eye. There's a definite refusal from all but one, who looks at me. She is not gesticulating or looking away. I walk right up to her and she remains still as I take the picture from a distance of about four feet. Despite all the material concealing her face, I sense that she is looking straight at me. Afterwards the women laugh and there is no sense of affront because this one woman did not mind.

Further along we come upon a glass-blower. He is skilful and showy, used to working before admiring strangers, the dazzling orb at the end of the long funnel in his mouth holding them in thrall. He has made ships, schooners with gauzy masts and sails spun like webs into forms of bony grace. There are glass camels, complete with detachable leather saddles, and the inevitable rows of sphinxes and pyramids, all different sizes.

"What percentage lead?" Sam asks the man.

He does not stop working, his cheeks puffed like smooth rubber, his forehead beaded with sweat. "Verry leetle," he calls over his shoulder.

In this particular light, the glass pieces refract well.

"Want one?" I say to Sam.

He smiles, considering his options like a child set loose in a toyshop.

"Why not? Might as well."

"I'll get it. Which do you want?"

"A ship," he replies without hesitation.

I turn to the glass-blower and ask him to pack it carefully. Sam seems surprised. We are not gift-buying types, have never imposed minor surprises on one another. Flowers perhaps, at birthdays or anniversaries. Books from me to him at certain times. But Sam has always bought his own glass. He knows I have an aversion to crystal of the conventional kind, although a certain fondness for his lead crystal collection has grown grudgingly.

161

"Thanks," he says awkwardly.

He stands beside me with his hands in his pockets. Such an uneasy soul. In this environment it becomes easier to forget certain things, to hope for change. The glass-blower calls out in Arabic to a child helper after the bartering is done and we have settled a price. The boy scuttles off and reappears with boxes and soft filling. The glass ship is laid carefully on a base in the largest of these boxes, a polystyrene and paper mixture is poured around it until the ornament is secure. Then the box is sealed and wrapped. The boy has fine little hands with straight, even-jointed fingers which work nimbly with bits of ribbon until the packing and wrapping is complete. He hands it to me and I pass it to Sam.

At the Palestine night-club the air smells of jasmine and smoke. The place is low-ceilinged, with thick walls and small square windows on three sides. Musicians and a belly-dancer will perform on a stage at the centre. We sample the local cuisine, succulent pieces of white fish and marinated artichoke hearts, followed by crumbling sweet pastries.

"Glad we came?" he suddenly asks, taking my hand.

Of course I'm glad we came, I tell him, wishing we could stay on. I resist telling him that I would be gratified if a slab of precast concrete were to drop from the sky on Sandrine during our absence.

"One always feels refreshed after a break," I comment in neutral tones

"You needed it," he says.

"So did you, my dear, even if you didn't realise it."

Whether it is the effect of the wine, or the heat, I have begun to feel angry. The musicians whirl on to the circular platform in the centre of the club. They're making such a racket that I can't hear his next words but his expression is inscrutable.

"We need to make a few changes," I say, moving nearer to him.

The musicians have begun to play. The sound is wild and exhilarating; the drummer's hands flash furiously.

"How? When?" Sam replies sleepily, taking a swig from a glass of beer. His eyes rest on the music-makers, then drift vaguely around the room.

"When we get back of course."

Restraint is tiresome. I am forever holding back, not letting go, inhibiting the full effect of what I really want to say.

"There are a few things we need to sort out at home, darling. No point denying it, Sam; we've got problems."

He doesn't answer.

"Did you hear me?"

"I heard you."

"You never listen."

"I heard you; I heard you!" he groans.

A dancer appears, all white teeth and waving arms. Exactly the kind of distraction we could do without. We are in the wrong place at the wrong time for this type of conversation.

"What do *you* want?" he asks suddenly, looking up. His eyes are on fire, angry and resentful. The woman is overweight and olive-skinned, her face dark and magnificent, the bone-structure proportioned and chiselled. In contrast, her breasts, stomach and hips wobble, but she uses her hands with grace. Despite some initial irritation, I am transfixed.

"I want to live with you," I answer, avoiding the issue. "What do *you* want?" I counter, hoping for a similar reply.

"I want to carry on as we are," he says quickly.

"Meaning?"

"Well," he blusters, "I suppose we could try harder to be a bit more — I dunno — I suppose we need to, say, spend more time together?"

Our mutual evasion almost amuses me. Can we keep it up much longer? Can it possibly go on like this for years? Are we so inarticulate, so without courage, that this is the lie we shall choose?

The thing must be said.

"We spend a lot of time together, all things considered," I begin.

"Yes, well, I want to carry on like that—at least—"

"Carry on! Carry on?" I guffaw in his face. "That's it all right: you want to carry on as *you* are, no decisions, no strings, no commitment to either *her* or me! Bastard. That's right, I *know*!" I hiss, throwing my drink in his face. Sam has gone white. As he wipes his face incredulously, his eyes seem smaller, his lips closed. He has genuinely not known that I knew. He sits shocked and still. The music grows frantic, there are wrist-bells and baubles, tambourines, reed-pipes and flutes. The woman's body whirls and gyrates, her flesh wobbles, her neat hennaed feet spin and her gauzy pantaloons and navel-jewel catch the light.

"What are you talking about?" he stalls.

"You know damn well what I'm talking about."

He wipes his forehead and neck with a handkerchief. The people at the next table are watching us.

"Let me tell you something, darling one," I start again with as much spite as can be mustered, "while you were cavorting around the house, while you had *that woman* in our bed and God knows where else, I was with Bill Bardon."

My voice is triumphant. Sam would like to beat me with his fist. Now that the words are uttered, I am ready to leave, but he catches me by the arm first.

"Get outside, bitch." he snarls between his teeth.

We rush outside as if to fight to the death. All the way back to the hotel we contend like cats. I match him easily when it comes to name-calling. People make way for us on the streets, step hastily past us, pass amused remarks as we stumble and argue. *Bollocks. Bastard. Pig. Prick. Selfish shithead. Ignorant dickhead.*

"How dare you call me a bollocks?" he practically screams as we pass a pastry-vendor. "You're off your rocker, bats in the belfry, neurotic — I can't stand it any more, Hanna — "

"Off my rocker? Neurotic? You've a nerve to talk about neurosis in your situation — "

"What exactly do you mean by that? Of course that's a red herring if ever there was one — you're diverting me from the main point as usual, you neurotic bitch, you and your fucking kinky relatives, what a crew, Jeeesus Christ, I've put up with them all this time, a crowd of drumlin-hoppers who think they're something special! A crowd of pig-ignorant provincials, that's what they are — "

"No more or less than yourself, you two-faced prick, so leave my family out of this. You're the one that's neurotic anyway, you fucking bastard, you're the one that can't admit he's sterile. S-t-e-r-i-l-e — got it? And instead of admitting it, you have to go *hooring* around with that fucking French *cow!*"

We're both screaming at the top of our voices just around the corner from the hotel. Each time one of us says something, we punctuate it by rushing ahead a few yards as if the last word had been uttered.

"And what have you been doing? Leading the life of the virtuous? Taken holy orders, have we, a vow of chastity? Oh no, you have to open your legs to one of your cockeyed relatives; *Cousin* Bill the family fairy — you didn't know that, did you, Hanna? That's right, the family fairy, or to be specific the old AC/DC, but bent as they come, camp, bum-boy, whatever you want to call it — " He begins to stammer, saliva bubbles at the corners of his lips. "How you could let yourself

165

get into a situation like that is beyond me! It's incest, you silly bitch, incest for Chrissake and you have to go scurrying off to the West to do it."

"I didn't scurry and it wasn't as straightforward as that—" I am flustered, grappling with the discovery of Bill's sexuality, trying to conceal my rage at not even suspecting.

"I swear, Hanna, I can't go on, can't take any more of this. Your opinions! The things you want to do! The things you don't want to do, I mean I thought we were living together to share things, but you've made it abundantly clear that you despise me, that I bore you. You don't love me and I can't take that," he says finally, in a lower voice.

"You have never bored me!" I roar. "That is one thing you have never done!"

We rush into the hotel in silence and up the stairs to our room. The stairway etches itself in detail on my mind as we hurry up, our anger still unspent. The green carpet, ornate mahogany banisters with little brass sphinxes, fronded plants in earthy urns on each side of the landing, woodcarvings and low yellow lighting, the warmth, the perfumed air.

"Well, what are you going to do?" I shriek in the hotel bedroom. "Marry her? Make an honest woman out of her? Do the decent thing?"

"Maybe that's just what I'll do! I just might, indeed I might!" he lashes back.

"Over my dead body will you have that—*whore*. I whisper, lowering my voice deliberately.

"You can't stop me—divorce or no divorce—there's not a thing you can do about it!"

"This is all because we have no children—you realise that, don't you?" I begin to sob, swept with self-pity and desolation. "And because you're bitter and bored with me!" I wail again, muffling my voice with a pillow.

"Yes, I am bored. You never leave off, do you, Hanna?" He has become more articulate and hard-hitting again.

"Why should I? You've never had so much as a sperm test done, you selfish donkey. You've never fully accepted that you're possibly s-t-e-r-i-l-e!" I spell again.

His voice rises. "That kind of thing isn't my department."

"It's both our departments!" I yell.

"It has nothing to do with me. You'd better get used to the idea; there's nothing I can do."

I try to placate him. "Don't you want to? Won't you even do it for me?"

"Why should I do anything for you when you've been — how long has this thing with Bill gone on — shacking up with the gay family artist. Was he a good lay, Hanna? Did it make any difference?"

"You have a nerve!" I whisper yet again. "None of this might ever have happened had things been more honest between you and me."

"Honest?" he finds the word comical.

"It happened just once," I say dully, flopping down on the bed, "which is neither here nor there anyway when you've been carrying on with *that woman* for far, far longer. Coming home to act out the part of the organic gardener-husband!"

"Bitch," he says.

"Bastard," I reply.

We observe one another from opposite sides of the bed. It is a long look of calculation. My blouse is open and my skirt undone. His shirt is torn at the shoulder where I pulled at it out in the street. The first glimmer of something bordering on humour begins to dawn. Suddenly we break up with laughter; suddenly we roll onto the bed and howl loudly, relievingly, as if we'd just discovered the funniest thing ever. We're filled with uproarious humour for perhaps five minutes, roll against one another. He whacks my bottom and I thump his shoulder good-humouredly, madly. But the mood changes again. Gradually, seriousness sets in and finally we no longer laugh but weep. The comical whacks have been transformed to slaps, to hurting pinches and thumps to bare flesh. I raise my left hand and slap Sam's face as hard as I can until I burst with sorrow for all our mistakes. He gives me a resounding blow on the thigh, his face contorted. I slap him again and he shrinks back. We have made a great admission and there can be no going back; both of us are sobbing incoherently as we turn from one another.

Eventually we sleep but separately. My head blazes with pain and I drift into unpleasant nightmares stamped vaguely with Sandrine's face. For the first time in my life, I awake wishing I were dead. Sam slumbers on the couch on the other side of the room, his breathing heavy. The anger wells up again and I would like to kick him to death.

Three o'clock in the morning. A muezzin chants in the distance. The Muslim population is awake and praying. Let them pray for me then; let them utter words of solace for a crazy Irishwoman. The curtains are still. The night is still and through a chink in the shutters a scimitar moon is caught up in the black sky. Despite all kinds of horror, life goes on; the gods are prayed to.

The next morning he leaves for London. I decide to remain for the last few days of the holiday. It is over. *Finis. Finito.* End. *Críochnaithe. Beendet.* I stay in the bedroom all that day, aware of time passing slowly, watching light change gradually as the sun moves across the hours. I shower three times, lie naked on the bed and later on the cool tiles of the floor, humming to myself.

Alone, I attempt to occupy myself. Alexandria makes me uneasy. It is not so calming and romantic as Lawrence Durrell made out in the *Alexandria Quartet*, and the bastion of Allied security during the war is quite different today. For something to do, I take a bus out to El Alamein.

Beyond the city the landscape is stark and dusty; yet it seems that there can be no higher manifestation of man-made balance than in Egypt. Those dense forms, stone stacked high in pyramidal shapes, obelisks still standing after thousands of years! The odour of jasmine in the bus signals Ramadan. Muslims are fasting and the sweet scent is supposed to stave off hunger pangs. I think of Sam as the bus jolts along. We have handled things badly. I should not have insisted on staying behind. Not that he asked me to accompany him home but I should have taken some stand, should have fought for him all the way. Instead, I have coiled back on my own blind anger because he said he was bored.

I have never thought of myself as boring, although it's an easy judgement I sometimes make on others, and one which I dispensed to Sam. Impatient, yes; impulsive at times, though passably controlled where necessary, easily angered, unwilling to give those I see as dullards a chance. But who ever admits to the possibility of being a bore? I attract the cross-grained like moths to a lamp. They know I will listen, those misfits and sufferers who sense the sinner in me. The people who like me rarely respond to Sam, find him austere and slightly intimidating. He unnerves the vulnerable, though, as he would say, that's their problem and not his. We cannot be entirely responsible for other people's reactions. But now Sam finds me boring. Obsessive too, he said. He has denied and denied the existence of a situation which has, as a result, grown to gargantuan proportions.

The bus lurches along, past rows of limp poplars, scrubland and lichen-coloured olive-trees. There are small brown goats herded by child shepherds who wave at the bus.

169

The absence of progeny dogs humanity like the darkest curse. To be made barren, to be unmanned, to be cut at the loins is the ancient word-wish of warlocks, of bitter peasants whom people feared. It is to be cut at the root like a *bonsai* tree, unable to flower to largeness.

We finally pull in on the westbound road. The passengers ahead disembark slowly. Some of them are country people loaded with sackfuls of vegetables. One woman carries a large speckled hen under her arm. It jerks its head from side to side, the long, clawed feet curled tightly beneath.

At the rest-house a boy proffers a trayful of black tea. "Shai?" he calls. Men and women grab the small tea-glasses without hesitation, slug relievedly in the shade. I too help myself, hear him mutter sullenly about baksheesh. I fumble in my bag, present a few coins which he proceeds to examine before smiling in acknowledgement. The tea is saturated with sugar and has been boiled.

The others shuffle into the inside rooms and I follow. Occasionally they cast a slow look in my direction, betray curiosity at the sight of a western woman travelling alone. Apart from that I am left in peace. I accept the food that is served at a small table covered in greasy oilcloth. Hot, spicy tomato soup, thickened with oval-shaped grains, followed by stuffed vine-leaves. I also order a beer to stanch the lingering taste of the black tea. It arrives huge and frothy but lukewarm.

The place reminds me of the old tea-rooms in Clonfoy which were visited mostly by people from outlying country areas and provided plenty of sweet tea, buttered bread and jam, and buns with sticky pink icing. The place would be packed after a fair-day, when the street outside was slimy with cow-dung and men spat gobs of spittle on the footpath.

Here the men and women eat separately and the air fills with the ricochet sounds and sibilant Arabic. For the hundredth time I promise myself an extra-mural course in modern Arabic, then break off surprised that I could plan ahead so spontaneously. I pay the bill, tip with immoderate largesse and leave the rest-house.

El Alamein is full of cemeteries and it dawns on me just where I am, why the place seemed vaguely familiar at the outset. Uncle Marius. Uncle Marius writing home in 1942 just a few months before he died, his simple observations about swallows and the things people wore, and the gemstones he'd said Aunt Florrie would like. I head back down the road, past what looks like some kind of museum and eventually reach the British cemetery. It is important to photograph this place. I am haunted by the presence of death.

Row upon row of simple gravestones stretch ahead. I follow each one from side to side. All are the same. Trees fringe the perimeter of the cemetery, and beyond lies the desert and its secrets. Afternoon sun beats relentlessly. A few tourists like myself stand and stare. There is little else to do.

We are uniformly dumbstruck, our intellectual sympathies replaced by a harrowing awareness, the bluntest of emotions. Horror and fear. Marius's body was never recovered. My grandmother kept his letters, his old school scarf and a pair of black, polished boots.

I retrace my steps as far as the stone archway on the walls of which the names of those who went missing are engraved, and raise the camera, feel my way through all those names with the viewfinder. Thousands of New Zealanders fell between 23 October and 4 November 1942. Like Uncle Marius they were all young. The camera skims the lists, an avid rectangle of names, ages and dates. Then I find it. *Marius Bardon, 18.* I stare and stare through the viewfinder at this bizarre link from a past never encountered, wonder what happens to the young and the good who are butchered and maimed. Where do they go? It isn't enough to say that if there's nothing on the other side of death, then you've got nothing to worry about. Equally, it is impossible to assume a location, a meeting of minds in some state of unimaginable bliss. But that is what I wish. There must be some sign that Marius lived. Something to justify his existence beyond five inept letters which my mother inherited and familial platitudes. Who will justify our existences when we die? Who will be able to trace something to Sam or to me and find meaning in that process?

I lower the camera without taking a picture, remembering how Kate used to tell Rose and me about the Bardons and the war. It seemed so exciting. Life stretched ahead like a road unfurling to bright light. The past was already written up, a definite adventure story told by people who had infinite freedom to do what they wished, whose function was to entertain the young and provide skeins of information on the world and its ways.

They have all changed, fallen like flies before my eyes — aunts, uncles, cousins. Sam and I are in the front line now, face mortality as never before. How can we, who have so little time, learn the secrets of history, do more than repeat mistake after mistake? As if the flawed act, the unthinking moment is the sole thing to be accepted? Is that the truth?

Back in the city, my calf muscles have begun to cramp. At the hotel I request salinated water to be brought to my room, then lie in semi-darkness for a while. I must go home, pick up the pieces. Beyond the bedroom window a whole world goes about its business noisily and energetically. That's the way to do things! To hustle and bustle, shout and laugh and cry and pick up the pieces again and again if necessary.

Saturday finally dawns and I am happy to leave Egypt. I have lost weight in the heat and look forward to cool, clear air and no dust.

"You take it easy, Meesis Troy!" one of the hotel waiters calls out as I pause at the reception desk before my departure. I nod, promise that I will, thank him for his kindness in providing me with weak tea and sweet fudge at the drop of a hat and tip him.

The airport is hectic. I lose my way twice, needlessly, before finding the appropriate gate. I am apprehensive about meeting Sam. I do not know whether he has tried to contact me and I have made no effort to phone. Later, on the plane between Heathrow and Dublin, a man tries to engage me in conversation. His voice is soft and Irish, though his vowels have been slipped. He wears a gold wedding band, a financier of some sort.

"Been on holidays?"

"Egypt." I am not in the mood for small-talk, will try to short-circuit his efforts.

"Hot, was it?"

"Very."

After some minutes spent reading *The Financial Times* he tries again.

"Myself and the wife avoid the Middle East. Bit risky y'know, bugs and whatnot, never mind the tricky politics."

"Risky." I echo in agreement.

"They could blow the lot of us sky-high!" He regards me for an instant, then blunders on. "Took a trip to Tunisia once—damn nearly died of dysentery—left a few cracked porcelain lavs in our wake!" he chuckles.

I laugh spontaneously at the thought of him and his wife shitting their guts out, vying for bathroom space.

"Damn doctor expected us to inject ourselves and eat nothing but carrot soup for three days, as well as drinking two litres of water every day."

"You must have felt like Gunga Din!" I have heard of

173

these resort doctors. French-speaking, casual medicos who spend their summers treating Europeans for gastro-intestinal disorders.

"Gunga *who*? Anyway, it was rather unfortunate."

"No wonder you won't risk Egypt then," I say, and hope he'll shut up. To my surprise he does, after reaching across to get a gin and tonic from the stewardess.

Ireland is cloudy. As the plane shudders down the airways from lacerating blue, through what seems like miles of whiteness, until Dublin is spread beneath in a rubble-edged crescent, I wonder if Sam has remembered my arrival. Then we're circling fields and hedges. Crops. North County Dublin flats. One final field, then the last drop on to the runway, the thunder of airbrakes and a measured taxiing towards the heart of the airport.

There's no delay at customs. I have nothing to declare. My left thigh is still bruised where Sam slammed his hand into it in Alexandria. I wonder if I hurt him sufficiently to leave a mark. I glance rapidly around the arrivals lounge. He is there, bearing flowers, a conciliatory smile on his face.

"How are you, darling?" he greets, embracing me fully.

He smells fresh and lemony, the coarse material of his jacket is oddly comforting as my cheek brushes his shoulder. I blink, amazed at the transformation. Perhaps sticking it out in Egypt gave him something to think about.

"I'm fine. Just fine."

"Good to see you again," he says.

"Yeah?"

"I was worried. I phoned through but you were always out. So they said."

Whether it is true or not, I am pleased.

To hell with the tests. To hell with him having them done. He's here and he's with me.

Chapter Twenty-Five

—w—

But after four months the new openness changes nothing. We live together in a mood of pleasantness, making obvious efforts to renew ourselves. He accompanies me on the odd shoot and takes an interest in my darkroom activities. He is particularly keen on a long-term commission on late twentieth-century urban architecture, selected prints from which will eventually go into a publication called *The Great Book of Houses*.

I hear little of Sandrine and, despite all the work at the practice, Sam does little overtime in the evenings; he is more likely to be at home with me or playing tennis with Tony. Perhaps the worst is over, I tell myself; perhaps the affair has spun itself out and Sandrine is being allotted less and less time.

Bill Bardon calls frequently on the phone and we chat for ages about nothing. He never quite got over my taking-off from the island, leaving him asleep, any more than I have recovered from the revelation of his gayness and my own lack of awareness.

"Does it make any difference?" he asks one day.

"In itself, no—but it changes things too," I tell him. "I can't for the life of me understand why you said nothing!"

"I'm sorry. I should have told you—it's just that you get used to saying nothing at all about yourself when you come home." He breathes out slowly, his voice rasping down the telephone. "Anyway, maybe I have the best of both worlds..."

"Maybe you have."

Had things worked out as I'd hoped after returning from Egypt, I'd have had a total reconciliation with Sam: Sandrine would be a thing of the past. As it turns out, I discover that he sees her at weekends when I drive off to visit Dan; I can tell by the care with which he attends to his clothing on Fridays, by those long, self-appraising looks in the mirror.

One morning, I rise with a new sense of determination, walk the length of the house to Sam's room to tell him that I'm leaving for good. I sit groggily on the edge of his bed in an old red T-shirt, observe him as he shaves through the open bathroom door.

"I never know how serious you are when you say things like that," he says through his teeth, taking a swipe at his throat with the razor. I feel like giving him a hand at it.

"That works both ways. Do *you* know how serious *you* are about anything?" I retort quickly. "Well, as I said, I'm leaving and I mean it."

He stands there for a split second, looking back at me from the mirror, one half of his face white with shaving-foam. "You know your own mind on that best, then," he says.

It's the day when his new building is to be officially opened. He's absorbed with appearances and slaps a few palmfuls of *Egoïste* on face and neck, steps back into the bedroom and inspects his trousers for specks of dust before hauling them on energetically, as if I wasn't there.

"Do you love her?" I ask.

The bed hasn't been changed since after we came from Egypt. Yet the eye notices examples of minor neglect in times of crisis. Chipped paint, cracked tiles, fungi growing in a corner of the landing where we never got the damp-proofing properly sorted out and because Sam had plans for a new-age house for us, modest in space but full of light.

"I don't know," comes the reply as he selects a red tie with navy spots.

If our generation had been subjected to a diet of the movies of the 1940s and 1950s we might handle relationships differently. For one thing, bald honest indecision would be unheard of. It would be a case of "Frankly m'dear, I don't give a damn" or "Maxim, darling, you mustn't ever leave me!" Either way, we'd all know where we stood and people wouldn't worry so much about taking responsibility for everything. It must be splendid to be able to let go of notions like that.

My announcing that I intend to leave is actually nothing more than a threat. A foolish one. I fear to move out alone, leaving Sam and home. I fear making way for Sandrine, will avoid that at all costs. Why should I make things easier for her? More than that, the simple truth is that I still *like* Sam Wright. I like him more than anybody else in the world, his thorniness, his awkwardness.

"I think I am leaving," I repeat, and this time it seems a possibility.

He ignores me. There is nothing unusual in this. Years before we married, I remember telling him that I'd kill myself if I failed my Leaving and he simply nodded. He didn't laugh or grow excited or tell me not to be histrionic. Nothing like that. Perhaps, after all, he has always accepted facets of my personality, more than I thought. Or perhaps he's just not capable of caring.

We leave the house together, I first. He follows after setting the alarm and checking some circuits near the patio windows. The garden is perfect. An Eden which Sam has created in the past months. The first summer freshness has long gone, the columbines have shrivelled, but tiger-lilies curl and flare, speckled and orange, and monkshoods and hollyhocks wave heavily in the light breeze. Mossy mounds of things I do not know the name of cluster on the rockery. In the morning, everything seems still and dewy. At times like this I imagine the whole world to be in a state of bliss, absolutely delighted with itself and its own infinite capacities.

He has taken to checking and rechecking the security system lately and polishes his lead crystal every evening, repositioning certain pieces. The glass ship bought in Egypt rests between a hedgehog and a rearing stallion, and like most holiday purchases has lost its initial brilliance in these northern parts where the light is muted. But he seems to like it. Sometimes he counts out loud. When I ask why he's counting, he denies having counted. When I insist that I heard him count to five at least three times, he shrugs his shoulders and raises his eyebrows. Even the glass pieces are aligned in fives, like miniature merry-go-rounds.

"What will I wear?" I call as an afterthought as he sits into his car.

"Dress up if you like," he says before revving up and taking off slowly.

I automatically decide to dress down that evening and go back into the house, undoing his precious security precautions to fetch a polka-dot slip dress. In the meantime I have a meeting at the office and a lunchtime street carnival to photograph.

Chapter Twenty-Six

—m—

The building is to be called the Cragg-Mortimer centre.

Already the local wiseacres and paparazzi have got to work naming it otherwise. Hubble Bubble. The Glass Palace. The Diamond as Big as the Ritz. It seems to float. Sam has created something magnificent.

This is of his mind, his dreams. It refracts light through lightly-arched steel buttresses, pentagonal glass panels on the overhanging upper storeys, even between the fine granite columns which flange the base at intervals. The river has been invited into this building. They have made an artificial canal which penetrates the ground floor and cellar level, which will be tidal like the river, and like the river quays, the walls will glimmer with opacity and water-shadow; there will be seaweed and mussels as the tide ebbs and flows.

People have arrived: inside there's a hum of voices and laughter; the smell of success is in the air. I make my way to where Sam stands with a foreign photographer, a contact of Sandrine's who plans to do a feature for one of the Parisian glossies. Beside them is the ground-floor centrepiece, a huge glass sundial. It is an impossibility in practical terms. The column is of delicately-fluted glass, the plinth beneath it cut with glass flowers, the dial itself equally transparent but with roman numerals etched into the surface. The little triangular marker is the only element in the design made of brass. It too is delicately wrought with tiny leaves and curlicues. Sunlight streams down from the huge glass dome above our heads, with its glass and steel cupola, and, as light rays strike the sundial, an image is thrown not only on to the flat surface of the dial itself but right down through the fluted base from where it is refracted radially. By some force of supreme art time cuts right down and splices the whole construct with a prismatic shadow.

This is our element, Sam's and mine. Glass and light. Left to themselves, all the chemical components and acids in the world are nothing without the imposition of a plan, an art. Those silicon dioxides, the soda ash, furnace temperatures of 1500°C are meaningless unless the mind's eye watches and creates, turns its attention on ways of redeeming the world and what we do to it, redeeming ourselves, through a vision of something better.

I want to put my arms around Sam's neck and cradle him and rock him as if he were my child. Foolish. I am absurdly proud of him, know by the set of his mouth that he is trying hard to contain his own feelings of delight.

"You've done it," I whisper.

"D'you think so?" It's not a question so much as a way of concealing emotion.

"I really do. It's the best you've ever done."

He nods his head. "It'll do. For now."

"I should think so."

The photographer stands to our left, waiting for Sam to finish with me.

"Ma femme," he informs him quietly.

We shake hands. The chap is toting a state-of-the-art Japanese model.

"Hanna Troy," he adds as the man arranges us for a shot.

He tells us to keep *tokking*, to *tok* away. But that is not our habit. The moment he issues the instruction, we clam up and the photographer looks disquieted.

"Okay-okay-okay-peut-etre un peu comme ça—oui, eh, encore, un peu, oui, ça va!" he fusses around, adjusting my head so that I am almost in profile but not quite. Not a word passes our lips.

"Dites quelquechose for Christ's sake," Sam says between his teeth, grimacing. We feel slightly ridiculous, standing there with what feels like elements of World War III exploding between us, while the photographer snaps at least twelve shots of us.

Sandrine hasn't shown up. At least she has some dignity. Sam will have told her that I know. Possibly he has even finished with her; perhaps the weekend was the last one with her. The dignitaries make speeches and people stand about angling their glasses, nibbling canapés. Around us the mullions rise up and up like graceful ribs, letting air and light into the building.

Anna, Mark and Tony surround me. Tony stands beside Sam, pleased with himself. Another photographer quietly closes in on them, captures both as they murmur chummily during the Minister's speech. Anna is hugely pregnant now and shifts uneasily from leg to leg.

"Big day, what?" Mark nudges me.

I mumble a reply.

"Chilly in winter though!" he jokes, nudging me again. "Next thing, Sam'll be building housing estates like this—" he tries again. "Homes for the great unwashed."

"Possibly. You never know quite what Sam will do next!" I respond primly. I want to hear the Minister, to catch every morsel of official praise and high-flown rhetoric directed at Sam. Anna moves closer.

"How was Egypt?"

"Great. Tell you later."

She ignores this. "Heard Sam got gippy tummy."

"Hmmm—it was very hot."

"Maybe we'll get away next year—divide the kids between Mark's mother and my sister for a while."

"You should—you can't beat a break on your own," I tell her, hoping to convey an impression of togetherness which I do not feel, although she must know about Sam and the Frenchwoman.

"It's lucky for you. No kids. No commitments—well—" She changes tack as I turn and look at her.

"You're jealous!" I say.

"Probably," she replies, unoffended. "Yes, I very likely am jealous," she continues. Her frankness disarms me.

"Well, don't be. It's not worth it."

Moments of split-second premonition occur from time to time. It's something which happens to drivers, the moment when you decide not to overtake another vehicle because you know—you just know for certain—that an articulated truck is about to come careering around the next bend on the wrong side of the road. In the same way I knew the day before Kate's death, correctly anticipated her passing even though she seemed quite well on that particular evening. It's a combination of sequences mixed with intangibles which suddenly build to an instant of recognition.

I know Sandrine is about to arrive, about half a minute beforehand sense her about to enter the sunny portals of the glass palace and make her way across to the sundial.

In she sails, cool and languid and ordinary. Lovers are seldom as we imagine. You know at a glance that they eat, sleep and excrete just like everybody else, that they occasionally have bad breath and that they also fart. They do not plan a campaign from on high and then move in on their prey. Her ordinariness is no consolation. If she were a voluptuous creature with deformedly large mammaries, it would be more bearable. But her demure coolness and that pleasant and benign face are an affront, because I cannot dismiss her out of hand. She is human.

We greet one another stiffly. She has made her way to the front of the crowd, stands behind Anna but at my elbow. After all, she had some input to the design of the great edifice and is responsible for the ventilation system, an innocuous miracle sandwiched within each floor. The building is a series of glass rings which rise around the central dome and cupola, each one supported by elegant mullions. I focus my attention on a piece of steel which curves along the first-floor struts. There is no point saying much beyond basic civilities. I am not going to pretend that nothing has happened, any more than she is.

"How are you, Hanna?" she asks carefully.

The French accent is less pronounced than on the previous occasion we met. She has learnt to aspirate. She is not quite sure just how much I know. Typical of Sam to keep her slightly in the dark. He does not mean to be casual about these things. His work absorbs him greatly, his obsessions occupy a great deal of thought, which is the excuse most people use in relation to errant lovers.

"Fine."

An image of Sam and Sandrine flashes into my head. If I entertain it, I'll pole-axe her. I glimpse the tangle of limbs, hear the voices, the cat-calls, recall the steamy damp air as they stumbled from the shower and left it running while they fell into the bed. There is absolutely no reason to be pleasant. She has taken what was mine, even if I'm not so sure how greatly I value what was mine. Sam is inadequate. He is a louse. The kind of man women are well advised to steer clear of. It is

183

possible that I have been wasting my time with someone who isn't worth a toss. An airhead, incapable of facing the truth about himself. A spoilt, self-absorbed dunderhead.

Again, our eyes meet and mine are unsmiling, the light dies in hers and she surveys me. Sandrine is a self-possessed woman. Clearly, she sees nothing wrong in the arrangement, has no fear of confrontation, has claimed Sam. Continental women learn one thing about men at an early stage in life. They expect them to philander, so when it happens it's not a complete catastrophe: they can treat it lightly. She turns to Anna and they begin to talk. Everybody claps as the Minister winds up. There are more photos, this time of Sam, Tony and the Minister as he cuts a glossy green ribbon drawn across the entrance to one of the ground-floor suites. More applause. More laughter. The mood of the crowd has loosened up considerably; little groups can be heard braying and exclaiming as they wander around the area inspecting this or that aspect of the design. People peer with curiosity down into the canal, pushing and shoving as they wait for the moment when the outside locks are opened and the water rushes in.

"Right, who'll press the button?" says Tony, looking around. People back off, unwilling to be the centre of attention. Sam moves forward. "Here. Let me. Let's have done with it!" he says, bending efficiently towards the control unit from which the electrical system is operated.

There's a hush for some moments, then a surprised babble of voices, of delighted oohs and aahs as the river floods in through the locks, rapidly engorging the canal. We remain gazing down, enthralled. Finally, the water settles into a slow, tidal rhythm, and our faces are reflected in a wobbling mosaic of shifting colour.

"It's a great occasion for us, no?" Sandrine says amicably to Anna, somewhere behind me.

"I suppose it is," Anna replies indifferently. I turn, she looks at me and now I'm sure that she knows everything.

"Sam and I—and Tony—" Sandrine falters, "we think of nothing else for months."

"I can imagine," says Anna, droll as you like. "When did you begin to plan it? The building—" she goes on, and I suddenly find more mischief in myself than I'd thought could exist. Sandrine is startled.

"Oh—let me think—" She shrugs her shoulders, draws her lips down and calculates. "Two year ago perhaps. He designed it two year ago."

"Sam drew up the basic idea five years ago, if I remember correctly," I butt in. "After a visit to Sweden, he came back all talk about light and snow and refraction."

Sandrine says nothing. She looks thoughtful. The reality of our shared past is possibly dawning on her, our years of planning things in a vague way, our dawdling over ideas and notions, all those subterranean links notched up with the things we'd lived through.

"I remember!" Anna says. "God, you both looked fabulous when you got back from Stockholm, just wonderful!"

"Every relationship needs new stimulation. I am sure Sweden was good for you," Sandrine interjects philosophically.

"Is that so?" I remark.

I try to suppress my rage. So. She imagines herself rescuing Sam from an unstimulating relationship, and there is little I can say by way of rejoinder.

"One doesn't have to go abroad to find stimulation, Sandrine," Anna replies icily.

All around us people move and jostle towards trays of food, drinks and champagne. Hungry and angry, I push towards a waitress for a couple of vol-au-vents, find myself beside Sam again. He turns around. Perhaps my expression

185

has altered, but whatever he sees in my eyes gives him such a start that he nervously jolts his drink to one side, spilling it with a lightning splatter on the Minister's suit. I stand stock-still, as if observing him clinically, from a distance.

"Are you all right?" he asks in some irritation.

"Yes. Sorry."

Then my mood changes abruptly. "In fact I'm so all right that by the time you get home I'll have packed your things."

The Minister shrinks back discreetly, pretending not to have overheard the exchange, and begins to mumble with Tony.

"We'll talk later, Hanna," Sam says in managerial tones.

"We won't talk—it's too late."

Sandrine and Anna are behind, I can hear their voices. Sandrine sounds angry, indignant. Anna has said something about Sandrine coming all the way over to Ireland to disturb other people's lives. The word "unfair" flutters around between them.

"Don't talk to me about things being unfair!" Sandrine snaps.

"I'll talk all I want!" Anna retorts. "You and your ex-husband in Fontainebleu—that's rich!"

"It's none of your bloody business to talk about my ex-husband!" Sandrine replies furiously.

"Well, pity you didn't stay with him and his damn dalmatians then!"

I glance quickly over my shoulder as they argue, then turn to Sam again. "Do you hear that? Are you listening to the pair of them? This is all over you!"

"What?"

"So you and your French bonbon can shag off wherever the hell you like!" I say.

The exchange is conducted in reasonably subdued tones.

People laugh and chatter, the well-fed and well-sired with drinks in their hands, the accomplished and talented, the not-so-talented but glad to be there anyway and the hangers-on. Nothing matters. I turn to make a grand exit, but halfway to the entrance Sam catches my arm. He is jittery, perspiration darkening the tips of his hair where it falls across his brow.

"Hanna, don't go—don't leave—I mean, look, I mean it Hanna, can't we talk later?"

I stare past him, cold to his nonsensical pleading. "I'm packing your stuff."

"Okay. You do that. I'll see you later."

"No you won't. I won't be in the house. You can pick your things up and be gone out of the place by nine tonight."

"But what are you going to do?" he whines.

"That's the first time you've ever, ever asked that, just when it's too late."

"Wait!" he calls, practically stumbling over his feet as I move on.

"The ball's in your court, Sam," I call nonchalantly over my shoulder. Again, the feeling of prescience, of the about-to-be-revealed, like eyes opened to new light. I am not about to escape, not yet.

"Sandrine is pregnant."

I run to the car, scream at him to get lost. He follows in the Morris Minor as I speed in and out of traffic, blowing the horn, mad to get home and be alone. Soon I lose him, vaguely aware of the shunting of other vehicles, horns, air-brakes squealing, diesel engines churning, motor-bikes, leather-clad couriers weaving in and out of the tailback. At the heart of our lives there has been terrible deception. Call it a mistake. Call it illusion. It is the worst thing imaginable. The child will bind them, hold them together as much as our childlessness drove us apart into icy, crystal compartments.

187

Either it's some fluke or else he isn't the father. I race through random possibilities, people Sandrine might have known rather well. The French photographer from the Parisian glossy, Tony. When did she last visit the ex-husband? Who else did she know over there? The trees throw shadows like blades on the motorway. It scarcely seems possible that the man with whom you've shared a life for years can turn out to be so different. He was going anyway. He had it all planned. Sandrine has had it planned. She was going to have him anyway. No contraceptive device could withstand it. Yet I do not believe that pregnancy was ever part of her intention. One of life's myths is that women lay a trap for men by getting deliberately pregnant.

My hatred has no limit. I pour the darkest afflictions on her. AIDS, VD, cancer, a heart-attack, a miscarriage — there is nothing good to be thought now. On the last stretch of road before our house, I concoct a possible death for Sandrine and finally understand the Japanese rationale of permitting workers ritually to punch and kick images of authority figures who have an unpleasant and intrusive say in their lives. If she could have a car accident or be shot, if she could die writhing, if she could just disappear off the face of the earth and let us get on with our lives!

People talk about men whose women make fools of them and the corollary applies too. My humiliation is complete. I have never been woman enough, have deceived myself all along. That is what people will say, though I am past caring what people will say, because people can only say so much and, having had their say, they are largely indifferent anyway. I burn. I burn. My body is still my sanctuary. What matters is to get away, find a bolthole, refuge, somewhere to lay my head.

"I'm sorry," Sam says when he comes in about twenty minutes afterwards. "Are you all right? I was afraid of an accident."

I refuse to look at him. Nothing can eliminate the deadness at the centre of life. All thoughts of packing his bits and pieces forgotten. Make coffee, take care to brew it rich and strong. Reliable. He sits on the edge of the kitchen-table as I move about, watching, his right hand rests on the back of a chair. We bought that table ten years before. It is rough and panelled, old beech. The little ridges and channels forged by woodworm years ago have been scoured. It was not new enough for Sam, he wanted a refectory-style rectangular table in black oak, then finally gave in and bought this one in a conciliatory gesture after an argument.

"So what next?" I say sullenly, pouring myself coffee. "Any more surprises?"

"I had no idea until yesterday," he replies.

"Why did you let me go there today? Why encourage me to come?"

"I — she wasn't supposed to be there — she was supposed to be with a journalist back at the office. He mustn't have turned up."

I sip the coffee with restraint, disregarding the careless lie.

"I didn't know. I just don't know how it happened," he carries on. I laugh bitterly, rock back and forth, holding my stomach. "Am I to take it, are you telling me it's really *yours*?" My voice is harsh, cynical. Mocking in the hope of hurting.

"It must be."

"How do you know? How do you know what that little wildcat gets up to?"

"Sandrine's not like that," he says.

"Sandrine's not like that!" I mimic. He's even loyal towards her, sounds almost noble, and mildly offended.

"Sandrine's not like that!" I mimic again. "Well, bully for her and here's to your mutual pleasure!" I sneer, flinging cup,

189

saucer and coffee-pot across the kitchen until the lot smash against the door.

Silence. The trickle of hot liquid, down walls, the door, along the edges of cupboards. Sunlight glides along the droplets, makes tiny prisms of the sodden mess around us. We continue to sit, nonplussed about the paternity of my husband's mistress's child.

"Hip, hip, hooray, buddy! You finally did it. What do we do now? Are you leaving, staying? Are we expected to share your favours now that you're going to be a *Daddy?*"

He rubs his hand across his forehead. "Hanna. No sarcasm. It doesn't help."

"You can stay or leave as far as I am concerned. Preferably the latter."

I've recovered fragments of dignity, turn and go upstairs. Again, the house floods through with silence. He is down there, pondering, wondering. How anybody can be so inept at dealing with his emotional life is beyond me. It's not as if Sam is stupid or uneducated; just that some vital, instinctive level of his personality remains only half-plumbed and maybe half-discovered through Sandrine.

I observe the garden from the bedroom window. Our beautiful retreat. I would not leave it for anything, for either of them. This is the place to be, my roots are here now, even if things have turned out poorly. Three types of beans grow in the vegetable plot; a few runs of potatoes every summer. They are white and floury and split deliciously when cooked. The raspberries are finished but there is garlic in abundance; there will be winter broccoli and coloured cabbages from China. I shall hire a gardener.

Sam always had the knack of capturing elements of the exotic. His commonplace tasks are made complex and rich with variety, and done with a singular ability to look out and beyond. That's part of the problem. He looks out and forgets about what's inside himself. The pregnancy will force him one way or the other. Either he will live with Sandrine or he will stay as remote as possible from her, like the swine he is.

Difficult though, seeing how she works with him. Can he sack her? Hardly. Can we share him? I think not. I couldn't stand it and sooner or later Sam would be driven out by the pressure of it all. No. He and Sandrine must decide what they will do and in the meantime I'll live here.

In late summer the evenings quieten; the birds are less excited; everything is long and mature, tawny and luscious. I turn from the window and lie on the bed. Perhaps the chemistry was wrong. Unresolved issues sometimes obstruct. Not a theory I set great store by, but all the same it makes you wonder. Why Sandrine and not me? She possesses what I would at one time have gone to any lengths for, what I pushed Sam for, the unreasonable bastard. Now she has something of his, and that is the only thing I envy, what they have achieved together.

I consider how I will live in the coming winter, imagine evenings by myself in the house. They do not frighten me, the thoughts of shorter days, of less light falling into the crevices of my life. If I want I shall be able to pass whole days in a state of dusk, the curtains closed, I shall be able to choose only as much light as is necessary to my equilibrium.

I fall asleep, into dreams; witness fragments of our lives and, inexplicably, strange, forgotten things from the past: the sight of Rose and Kate in the old kitchen at home, arguing. The words are unclear but their tone is vital, conveys itself by their movements. I doze again, torn by feelings of incredible loss. When I awake, Sam is in the room, stands over me.

"You were crying."

My face is wet. "So I was."

We stare at one another. At the back of it, the stirrings of some kind of forgiveness.

"I dreamt about home. About Clonfoy," I tell him.

Chapter Twenty-Seven

—∽—

Time to return to Dr Flynn-Mitchell. My pace quickens.

I want to arrive composed, not floundering in, late and in a dither. I do not want to give the impression of being a potential basket-case.

Some of the office workers head home along the Green, young people who still look busy and energetic. I'd like to wind the clock back ten years or more, to the time before the rot set in. When we could have taken control of the situation.

I have been to El Alamein and established that Uncle Marius did exist, that he really died in 1942. One story at least which has proved to be true, one with a definite resolution. Did we imagine some things? Who would think of putting up the hazel branches in our family now that Uncle Theo is dead? I decide to begin the practice again the following Easter, with or without Sam, wherever I am.

The world was a wonderful place on the day of the photograph at Rock Bog. I was supported on all sides, full of hope and the prospect of adventure and derring-do. Today, the hopes survive, though I am less sanguine about them. But I do not lack courage, am not so unnerved. The feeling is still within me. I remember the mountain-ash trees and the chill wind up on Rock Bog, then the heat of El Alamein, and the way Sam lashed my thighs with his hands that night in Alexandria. None of it, none of it, what I expected.

By the time I've mounted the stairs to Dr Flynn-Mitchell's room, the need to say anything has evaporated but I decide to see it through. The appointment is fixed, and she might help me make more sense of things, so that some of those vast, unexplored spaces might be inhabited.

Dr Flynn-Mitchell is a sensible woman, a neutral third party. She listens as I recount and she tells me nothing I have not by now figured out for myself in the course of the afternoon, but I promise her that I will come again in a month.

Nothing turns out as expected. The things I would like to tell Sam! The harmless secrets that have gone unshared. I would hold him close and never let him go. His lead crystal is laid out at home. I cannot claim that I keep the pieces as he would, but neither have I smashed them.

I am not waiting for him, even if the day comes, even if he eventually returns.

That evening I attend to one more detail. I am deliberate and patient, take my time when I return home, sit for a long time considering how I should look. Eventually, I set the camera up on the patio, on automatic, set myself in the sunny corner and let it shoot. The light is golden. My hands are folded in my lap, neither tightly curled nor completely flat. My cream cotton dress is smudged with chocolate just above the knee, there's a blob of dark red from the wine at the pizza-place, and my white jacket is stained with smears of blood from the time I rubbed it after pinching my hand earlier in the day. My make-up is minimal and a solitary hair sprouts on my chin, a fine, dark one which I pluck out every so often.

The camera clicks and clicks. I have begun to smile. The smile is my own. Inexplicably, for the first time in years I sense a great weight lifting and being replaced by lightness and airiness. I do not smile for Sam or Dan or Kate or Rose. I have praised them and the past, but enough is enough. In this moment I do not praise them. I am no longer anybody's good girl. There is nobody to please, rebel against, react to, nothing to live up to except myself.

Finally, I smile fully, for myself and my own life. I am young and I am healthy. Any loss cannot be worse than the losses already sustained in this war. I am Hanna Troy. That is what matters. He never will be the centre of my happiness again.

Never.

There is too much glass and light in Sam's head. His thoughts and ideas are of glass, furious and heated behind that diffident face. Hard, delicate as crystal. Nevertheless, I still imagine a lead-crystal house, mullioned and tall, where he and I could know something deeper, colder than flesh, our bones making contact as we sleep, our tortured dreams vaulting, Sam's glass palace, its floating sundial, its translucent shafts of light spanning the distance between our souls. These things are to be imagined, must rest in the realm of *perhaps*.

The camera clicks precisely, rhythmically. I relax completely as the shutter slides down and up, down and up, a neat blade giving shape to the moment.

– fin –

451
Editions

46805238R00119

Made in the USA
Middletown, DE
09 August 2017